The new post-Philby organisatio:
proving affective. Information wa:
But there was a new danger...
At the fag-end of the 1960s,
still reeling from the betrayals and defections of the Philby
era. Espionage is changing, with agents recruited on a
freelance basis – tiny, individual jigsaw pieces in a much
larger puzzle. One reluctant recruit is young Czech dissident
O.B. Blanc, on the run accused of murdering a KGB officer
and his mission to plant listening devices in a select London
gentlemen's club is anything but straightforward – or
gentlemanly. Reg Gadney's cynical and icily convincing
debut thriller, first published in 1970, was greeted with
acclaim by critics who suggested comparisons with the work
of Graham Greene and Franz Kafka.

Reg Gadney was born in Cross Hills, Yorkshire in 1941 and
educated at the Dragon School, Oxford and at Stowe.
Commissioned into the Coldstream Guards he served in Libya,
France and Norway, where he qualified as a NATO instructor
in Winter Warfare and Arctic Survival. He was subsequently
employed in the British Embassy in Oslo as Assistant to the
Naval, Military and Air Attaché. He then read English, Fine Art
and Architecture at St. Catherine's College, Cambridge and whilst
there he became the editor of Granta. He was awarded a
Theodore von Karman Scholarship to study at the Massachusetts
Institute of Technology where he became a Research Fellow. In
1969 he was appointed Deputy Controller of the National Film
Theatre and in 1970 became a part-time Tutor at the Royal
College of Art. He was subsequently made Senior Tutor, Fellow
and the youngest Pro-Rector in the history of the College. He
has lectured at Oxford and Cambridge, Harvard, MIT, the
Hermitage Museum in St. Petersburg and at the Academy of
Arts and Sciences in Moscow. Since 1970 he has written 13
novels, non-fiction and works of history. He devised and wrote
the 5-hour TV drama Kennedy *(1983) broadcast on NBC, which*
was sold to 50 countries with 27 of them broadcasting the series
simultaneously. The series was nominated for three Golden
Globes and four BAFTA awards and won the BAFTA for Best
Drama Series. He also adapted Iris Murdoch's The Bell *(1982)*
and Minette Walters' The Sculptress *(1996) for the BBC, which*
won him BAFTA, Writers' Guild and Mystery Writers of America
'Edgar' nominations. A respected painter as well as writer, his
latest one-man exhibition 'Portraits' opened in London in May
2014, his models including Helena Bonham-Carter, Sir David
Hare, Bill Nighy and Nicole Farhi. His work is represented in
private and public collections in the UK, USA, Canada, Norway,
Japan, Australia and New Zealand.

Top Notch Thrillers

Ostara Publishing's **Top Notch Thrillers** aim to revive Great British thrillers which do not deserve to be forgotten. Each title has been carefully selected not just for its plot or sense of adventure, but for the distinctiveness and sheer quality of its writing.

Other Top Notch Thrillers from Ostara Publishing:

DRAWN BLANC

Reg Gadney

Ostara Publishing

First published in 1970

Ostara Publishing Edition 2015

Copyright © Reg Gadney 1970

ISBN 9781909619319

A CIP reference is available from the British Library

Printed and Bound in the United Kingdom

Ostara Publishing
13 King Coel Road
Colchester
CO3 9AG

www.ostarapublishing.co.uk
The Series Editor for Top Notch Thrillers is Mike Ripley, author of the award-winning 'Angel' comic thrillers, co-editor of the three *Fresh Blood* anthologies promoting new British crime writing and, for ten years, the crime fiction critic of the *Daily Telegraph*. He currently writes the 'Getting Away With Murder' column for the e-zine *Shots* on www.shotsmag.co.uk.

to A

'Someone tells about men who in terrible crimes dedicate themselves to mutual silence.'

Kierkegaard

1

O. B. Blanc had never known his own first names. It was a curiosity he enjoyed, an eccentricity to do with names which he found that the English particularly appreciated.

He knew little of London and had he been offered more than one address to live at his first choice would not have been 6 Diadem Court in Soho. He had gone to an agency that advertised itself at the top of the Flats and Maisonettes Column in the *Evening Standard*. The flat in Diadem Court had been empty for several months. It was the cheapest they had in Soho. This was the district he had selected in his imagination in Prague, a district, he thought, which was the hunting ground of artists and writers, and its cafés would be like those under the tiled roofs in the narrow streets of Malá Strana. Instead there were slot-machine palaces, striptease clubs and myriad office complexes of film companies, overseas food importers and the tourists grabbing in the night.

He had three rooms to himself. Their previous tenants had been two prostitutes, or so he had been told by the owner of a delicatessen on the corner. The two girls, ageing a bit, had doubled up for company during slack mornings and economised by hiring one maid between the two of them. Then one of them had her arm broken by a middle-aged German. It would be a German, thought Blanc.

The flat had been half redecorated since they left. Most of the furniture had been replaced. But the narrow staircase was still covered by a stringy carpet which changed colour for effect as you reached the top floor.

From the outside the only visible changes had been the removal of the name plates—'Tessa', 'Sandi'. Upstairs Blanc

1

had blocked in the spy hole in the door of what was now his living-room.

Diadem Court was filled with the smell of roasting coffee beans.

Blanc was coming home.

He collected his mail from a rack just inside the door and climbed the awkward stairs irritably. It was a warm, humid day for so late in September and he was overdressed, so that his shirt stuck to him. When he reached the first-floor landing he hoisted a box file onto the window sill. Down in the courtyard he could see two tall striptease girls hurry past swinging cheap pastel-coloured vanity bags. One of the girls' legs looked white. Blanc imagined that they would be slightly bruised. The girls usually dawdled through the courtyard in the early evenings, first from one end from Berwick Street and when they had completed their work in Dean Street they came back from the other direction.

This afternoon they were in a hurry.

Blanc turned away from the window and climbed the last flight of stairs to his flat. It was as he had left it that morning. His bed was unmade and the bed clothes piled at the end of it. His striped sheets crumpled together forming a strange optical pattern. They had not been changed for three weeks. Some old shoe boxes containing tightly packed card indices lay on the floor, each with a red pencilled book reference at the top.

On the walls were some gold framed prints: one of a prize fighter, Tom Hickman, cut from *Boxiana*—'the gas-light man', the others of two girls in angular, rather acrobatic poses. Blanc thought they were Klimts. The most attractive was of a girl curled up on a background of bright patterned fabric. Her mouth was slightly open, and her hair fell across one exposed pink shoulder.

He undressed and got into his shower. The tepid water trickled down his back and he directed the jet onto his face. The water turned cold so he pulled the regulator from right to left but it made no difference. Wrapping a towel round his waist he sat down on his bed to read his mail.

There were three letters. One was a telephone bill for just

2

over six pounds, another was from the Fitzwilliam Museum in Cambridge about correspondence between a former director and W. Scawen Blunt—the subject of his research. The third letter was in an envelope marked Private and Confidential and Blanc read it with disbelief :

> Home Office
> Immigration and Nationality
> Department
> Princeton House
> 271 High Holborn
> London WC1

Dear Mr Blanc,
My Department has given the very closest consideration to your application dated 28 July. I regret to have to inform you that an extension to your Temporary Resident Visa (Special) (No.5936/AV/68) cannot be granted. The matter has been discussed at length with the appropriate department of the Foreign Office and it is not possible for the present allocation of such extensions to be exceeded. I do, however, feel that in the circumstances I should inform you of the considerations pertinent to your own application. These are as follows :
(1) It is noted that on the evening of 21 August 1968 you were party to acts of violence against an Officer of the KGB outside the office buildings of the Central Committee of the Czechoslovak Communist Party during the departure from those buildings of Prime Minister Černík, Dubček and several other leaders of the Czechoslovak Communist Party. It is also noted that you avoided arrest and subsequently organised demonstrations or participated in them during the last week of August 1968. It is further noted that you participated in several acts of sabotage (the details of which you informed this department of in your letter of 28 July 1969). This Department is not in a position to comment on your actions. The matter has nevertheless been examined in the light of the Soviet-Czechoslovak Treaty of 16 October 1968 (ratified by the Soviet

3

Praesidium and the Czechoslovak National Assembly on 18 October 1968) : Article 9, Paragraph 3. 'In the case of commitment of punishable actions against Soviet troops temporarily stationed on the territory of the Czechoslovak Socialist Republic, and also against persons serving with them, the persons guilty of such actions will bear the same responsibility as for punishable actions against the armed forces of the Czechoslovak Socialist Republic and persons serving with them.' I am to inform you that, in keeping with a Special Agreement, Her Majesty's Government is not able to contravene this article recognising as it does the present government of the Czechoslovak Socialist Republic. Therefore, I regret that the extenuating circumstances you listed in your letter accompanying your application and to which I have summarily referred above cannot be entertained by my Department.

(2) It is noted that on your arrival in this country a Temporary Resident Visa (Special) was allocated to you for a period of 12 months, and that Clare College, Cambridge awarded you a Junior Fellowship for three years to pursue a course of independent research on the papers of W. Scawen Blunt. It is also noted that you took up residence at Clare College, Cambridge for the Academic Year 1968-1969 and afterwards at 6 Diadem Court, London, W1 to pursue your researches at the British Museum. We have given consideration to your reasonable view that your researches would be considerably impaired in the event of the extension to your visa not being granted. However, as your researches are not leading to a Doctorate of Philosophy we regret that we are not able to consider the necessity for continuance as a further extenuating circumstance. We note that you applied to the University of Cambridge for consideration as a candidate for a Ph.D. but your candidature was not accepted. We are further unable to allow you an extension to make a further application for such candidature at a later date.

(3) We regret that we cannot entertain the extenuating circumstances dealt with in paras (1) and (2) above. I

feel I should nevertheless tell you that the overriding factor contributing to the rejection of your application is that the Allocation of Visas under the Student Exchange Agreement between the United Kingdom and the Czechoslovak Socialist Republic is fully subscribed. As from 1 January this year, arrangements for the granting of Temporary Residents Visas (Special) have been discontinued irrespective of the country of origin of the applicant. It is therefore not possible to grant you either an extension or a renewal of this category of visa. Finally may I draw your attention to the conditions of your present Temporary Resident Visa (Special) (No.5936/AV/68), more particularly to the Date of Expiry falling as it does 10 days from the present date. I feel that it would be appropriate to inform the Embassy of the Czechoslovak Socialist Republic (7 Palace Gardens, London, W8) of arrangements that you may make concerning your return. Perhaps you might approach Mr Jaromír Busek who I understand deals with matters concerned with repatriation.

> Yours faithfully,
> E. L. C. Greville
> (Immigration and Nationality Department)

Blanc stared out in front of him. He read the letter through again. 'My Department is not in a position to comment on your actions' : that must mean that the matter of the demonstrations would stay Private and Confidential. Neither Greville, whoever he was, nor anyone in his Department would 'comment' to the Embassy. Anyway, Busek was one of the few Czech diplomats who had stayed on in the London Embassy since the end of 1968 and it was known that his sympathies were ambiguous. Busek wouldn't pursue him, it would be a waste of his time. It would also be politically dangerous for Blanc's forced extradition to be bandied around in the English Press. But in Prague there would be a record of his commitment to the student organisations supporting Dubček's followers and it was certain that his activities during August 1968 would have been well documented by the Czech Security Services and the KGB.

The fellowship at Clare had only been awarded to him after

prolonged consultations with the Home Office, during the flood of goodwill towards Czechoslovakia which had now subsided. But once emotion cooled, a subsequent vaguely-worded policy of easing Anglo-Soviet relations was announced. At first it had been a convenient promise of the kind that sounded responsible and it had found a great deal of nationwide support. Times had changed and Blanc arrived at the natural conclusion—he would receive little sympathy from the Home Office. All of this indicated that Busek would be happy to get Blanc out of England and back to Prague with the least possible fuss.

Blanc realised that his list of extenuating circumstances had given little weight to his application, and had known that their inclusion would be something of a gamble. He could never have predicted the extent of official British goodwill towards the liberal elements in Czechoslovakia. He had deliberately left out certain aspects of his anti-Soviet activity during the last days of August 1968. But the present régime would definitely know that he had killed an agent of the KGB outside the office buildings of the Central Committee of the Czechoslovak Communist Party in Příkopy Avenue. Two of his friends from the Faculty of Literature, Jan Holotík and Josef Šmeral, had hidden him in a flat in Vysočany. From there he had attended one demonstration in Old Town Square and then he had planned several protest strikes at the Č.K.D. Factory in the Vysočany area. He had wanted to encourage the railway workers as well to embark on a prolonged strike which would have really hurt the Russians. But events had overtaken him when Holotík's sister who worked in the Communist Party offices discovered that the KGB were making very real efforts to find Blanc. Had Blanc's friends known that the armed forces and police were still uncertain of their instructions of 21 August they might have tried to get Blanc out of Prague sooner than they did. As it was they risked waiting until 30 August. At 11 pm on 30 August they persuaded one of the organisers of the newspaper distribution services to give them the use of a police car (these were being used to smuggle newspapers past the Russian check points on the bridges out of Prague). At Benešov, thirty miles south of the city, Blanc was transferred to a small van and five hours later crossed the border at the České Velenice check-point. At about six in the morning of 31 August, Blanc reached Vienna. He heard there that the KGB had arrested Holotík and Šmeral. That was the last he heard of them.

He had no difficulty in arranging a seat on a flight to London that afternoon, where, within four hours, he was introduced to an organisation set up by the National Union of Students to help refugee Czech students. From then on it had been a simple matter to arrange his appointment at Clare College, Cambridge. But although a number of dons had shown interest in his work, and indeed some surprise at the great deal of information on Blunt manuscripts that Blanc had gleaned from museums and private collectors in this country, the other research students had treated him with withdrawn condescension. Student unrest, which began soon enough at the start of October 1968 in Cambridge, provided little interest for him. As far as he could see the students had nothing to be disturbed about. He was haunted by the fate of Holotík and Šmeral and increasingly by anxiety about his own fate. No one else in the University of Cambridge could be wanted by the KGB and he dismissed an invitation to address the Cambridge University Communist Society as juvenile and tactless. He disliked the one party he went to which had been organised by the Chaplain of his college, and he rejected an invitation to join a Bible Reading circle. So an outsider might have concluded that Blanc had discovered very little about England during his year at Cambridge and the period in London. But he did get to know the other students on his staircase in Clare.

As time went by and he oscillated between a sentimental regard for Prague and furious outbursts against the Russians, his listeners were understanding, yet only one or two of them displayed affectionate interest in his predicament. However, his need for company was never strong, and by the end of the summer term his acquaintances greeted him apologetically. Fortunately, Blanc had already begun to be completely absorbed in his study of Blunt, which provided him with an escape.

He still hoped at the back of his mind that somehow he would be able to stay in England indefinitely. But now, his hope had gone. He had ten days left. Then he would be put on trial in Prague.

He bitterly regretted that he hadn't made any close friends in London. Just to talk over his predicament with someone would have helped. Preferably a girl, but he knew none. At home it would have been different because he fitted in. His circle of acquaintances accepted that he would take up a junior teaching post at the university and that was important to gain a girl's confidence in Prague. There was, or more correctly, used to be, a future. In London, he hardly knew how to begin. The only thing to do was to wait, to continue the routine at the British Museum and to tell the office at Clare which paid his grant that he was going home.

As his last week ended he found it hard to sleep. He lay awake wishing he could lose himself in London. He might become a London solitary bound by the hours of early morning picking fruit from delivery vans outside Covent Garden. He could join the shabby figures snatching pints of milk from doorsteps or simply hang around the rail terminals with the pale washed travellers coughing on their first cigarettes. There were solitaries such as this in Prague or any European city; but to join them was harder than one would have thought.

He desperately wanted circumstances to be different, but the inevitability of his predicament began to unnerve him.

With two days to go before his departure he paid his last week's rent and returned his rent agreement to the Agency. He bought a sea and rail ticket to Prague at Čedok in Oxford Street with the remainder of the grant and then, for the last time, at about midday joined the day's visitors to the British Museum.

2

He sat at a table in the North Library of the British Museum which he had begun to think of as his own. It had sometimes occurred to him that this streak of possessiveness was similar to that of elderly church-going spinsters who in their mind's eye, reserved and came to possess *their* pew. He argued that he, like the fragile spinsters, sat regularly in a building whose function was mainly cerebral, with objects generally considered spiritual. Or perhaps they were stimulants. In any case the church's contents like the museum's held the promise of revelation.

He watched the others come in: an Indian girl in a sari rustled past him to her seat. He wondered why she took no notes. Three men wearing different shades of sports jackets walked to their places. They were familiar to him as regulars. Two of them wore glasses with very dark rims running only across the tops, which, he supposed, was designed to give added authority by increasing the dark tones of the eyebrows.

He pored over his books and papers, crowding references and cross references onto three green-lined cards. *Blunt, Wilfred Scawen*, he noted, in brackets : (*MSS additional in Fitzwilliam Museum, Cambridge,—unavailable until 1972*) *But see 'The Love Sonnets of Proteus' (1880)*. Noon passed. The Indian girl swept out for lunch. One of the sports jackets was removed and a faint body odour filled the room. Books were brought in, others removed; someone was reminded not to lean on a folio.

He told himself in the early afternoon that he should stay there till the room was closed. The tables began to fill up, and the piles of books, papers and pencils increased. At about four a small piping voice could be heard at the main desk,

9

'Boehme's works, no, the reprint please. D. G. Barker's.' And then the monotones and calm voice of the girl at the Enquiry desk.

'I'm sorry we only appear to have various seventeenth-century translations. You'll find further entries cross-catalogued under Jacob Behmen. I think most of the relevant literature is being read at present.'

'Would you tell me when I might expect something to be available?'

Blanc could see the man's back. Wispy dry hair was combed straight back and was beginning to curl slightly over the collar. The man turned. Blanc looked down.

'I think it unlikely ...' the assistant's voice faded.

'But you see ... it really is rather crucial at this time....'

'Well you might ask ... the gentleman over there.'

Blanc looked up. The man was approaching him.

'Would you mind if I asked you when the Boehme material might be available to me?'

'You working on Boehme?' Blanc asked.

'I'm particularly keen to trace a copy of D. G. Barker's edition. Perhaps you could help me.'

'There isn't one here, have you tried the Westminster Library?'

'Their copy's on reserve and nothing would persuade the librarian to let me use it.'

Blanc looked at the man's eyes. They appeared glazed through heavy lenses, one of which had the effect of magnifying the left eye. He looked about forty, and his stiff collar was digging into his neck, leaving a red mark where it rubbed.

'What do you recommend?'

'I could let you look at my copy, it's rather special, a gift, so would you mind finding your reference at my place. I would lend it ...' Blanc at once regretted the offer.

'Absolutely. It's very good of you.' He held his hand out. 'My name's Barnes. Cyril Barnes.'

'If you'd come round this evening. About nine, 6 Diadem Court—just off Dean Street.'

'That's very good of you. I'd be delighted.'

The man pushed his glasses up to the bridge of his nose,

smiled and made his way out. Blanc liked Barnes's academic politeness. There was something safe about the enlarged left eye. It made him vulnerable. And they shared an obscure interest. He doodled on his reference card. Barnes would be his last visitor.

The anonymity of the evening crowds allowed him to feel safe, but made it hard for him to push his way along New Oxford Street and he became apprehensive: perhaps Busek would approach him before he left London and force him to fly straight back to Prague. This would make it impossible for him to hide out in Vienna. And Vienna was his last chance. Holotík's sister might still be there. It was a possibility even though she had left Prague shortly after himself. She knew her way around, though God knows how he'd find her.

'Get back.'

A bus swerved, car horns sounded in reprimand. He had stepped out into the traffic. A policeman was walking over to him. He launched himself into the people on the pavement with one shoulder forward.

Diadem Court was empty and he could see that his flat was in darkness. As usual the alleyway was slightly green in the yellow light. He walked past his flat and bought himself dinner at an Italian coffee bar in Dean Street. Afterwards he watched the pleasure seekers looking at the hoardings of a Sex cinema and a number of men scrutinising the window display of a shop for Books and Magazines.

If Busek tried to get him he would meet him at his flat. So at nine o'clock he approached Diadem Court with caution and for some time leaned against the boarded up doorway of a Church Welfare Centre. Barnes didn't come. He must have found his translation elsewhere.

He had no alternative. He couldn't afford a hotel. He'd just have to sit it out in his flat.

The stairs to his flat were in darkness because the bulb had gone. He could just feel his way with the aid of the banisters and as he reached his own landing the light from the hallway window showed him where he was going. He

11

searched for his keys; not in his coat, which he took off and slung over his arm. Not in his jacket. Then he remembered that, with Busek in mind, he had taken the precaution of pushing them down behind the lavatory cistern at the end of the hallway. It might have delayed things.

As he reached for them he noticed several cigarette butts in the bowl. Someone else had used it recently.

He pushed his key into the lock, and he realised that the door wasn't locked at all—the keys had been found, used and then replaced—the lights were on and his heavy curtains drawn. They let no light through to the outside. The back of his sprawling armchair faced him with its drooped rose patterned cover hanging loosely over it.

He could just see the top of a man's head leaning to one side, his arm lying flatly along the right arm of the chair.

It wasn't Cyril Barnes.

3

Blanc's chair, the one with the drooping roses, was one of his few personal possessions that had caused the others on his staircase in Clare to embark on flights of humour. The chair had not passed unnoticed by the don who was responsible for the allocation of college rooms to undergraduates. Just before Blanc's arrival in Cambridge the don had insisted that 'our Czech friend' should 'live in'. This was partly because the don had a mischievous interest in the private affairs of W. S. Blunt, and he suspected that the papers might reveal secrets of a sexual nature once they were made available to the general public. But the don hid his anticipation from Blanc, instead he said to him, 'I feel that having a Czech amongst us contributes to the international flavour of the college,' a flavour which was not immediately apparent to Blanc. However, when the don saw the chair, and recognised it as a reject from English suburbia (he was practised in such methods of recognition), he convinced himself that the extent of Blanc's contribution to college internationalism would, sadly, be negligible; and he subsequently avoided Blanc altogether. Except on one occasion, outside the Porter's Lodge: 'Ah, Mr Blanc,' the don exclaimed, 'Nemám žádné kapesníky!' (I haven't any handkerchiefs!) and he walked off in a hurry, chuckling to himself at a joke so obscure as to be without any meaning to Blanc whatsoever. Possibly, Blanc thought, he's been crying about the chair.

One of the men on his staircase liked the chair, and also knew something about Blunt. It was this much older man, Francis Smith, that he had engaged in some complex arguments about Czech nationalism. At the time Blanc used startling blue writing-paper with an equally vivid green ink

13

for the limited correspondence he had with museums and other research sources. Francis Smith had a year's 'leave' from the Foreign Service to pursue an Intensive Russian Course in Cambridge language laboratories.

When Smith first saw the ink and writing-paper one late summer night, it prompted him to tell Blanc that Major-General Sir Stewart Menzies, the former head of the British Secret Intelligence Service, had used exactly the same paper and exactly the same ink. There then followed a discussion of the S.I.S.; speculation about its present roles and development; and the theory of security in general.

Apparently Smith had been sent into Wormwood Scrubs to look at the mess left there by the M.I.5 in the 1940s. Smith had also known Philby, who had visited the Scrubs with a Commander Peters in 1940. Smith, it seemed, had joined the Communist Party as an undercover agent in the late '30s; and what staggered Blanc when he heard it, was that the S.I.S. had in fact known that Philby was feeding the Russians well before the Second War: 'the victim of the biggest counter-double bluff ever known' was how Smith described Kim Philby.

This discussion had been one of the very few that Blanc had ever had on any aspect of crime at Cambridge. He and Smith had often talked of political plots, their scales and relevance. But when he came down from Cambridge Blanc never saw Smith again. Perhaps he'd been given a minor post in the British Embassy in Moscow or some other Iron Curtain country. So, even though he was half prepared for Busek, Blanc was surprised but not alarmed to see Francis Smith get up from the armchair. 'You didn't mind me waiting in here?' he said.

'No. It's a surprise though.'

'I've tried to get in touch with you here all day. In the end I thought I'd just sit it out. In fact, I was beginning to think you'd run for it.' Smith spoke with authority and gave the impression of being larger than he really was. His hair was brushed hard against the sides of his head and thinning on top. His suit was of a light grey worsted. He was taking his time and Blanc tried to disguise the fact that his thoughts were racing. Should he tell Smith straightaway about his difficulty—or should he somehow seek his help?

Smith decided it for him.

'I've heard you're in difficulty with the Home Office.'

'How do you know?'

'All applications for visa extensions come through to the part of the Foreign Service I work for. We double check them. Yours was refused before it reached us. But eventually it ended up with me. Anyhow, briefly, I can find a way round it for you.'

'Do you mean that?' Blanc asked.

'I don't see why not. We discussed it this morning. You weren't to know but my subsection at the Foreign Office has had an interest in you since you arrived in London. The circumstances of your departure from Prague brought you under surveillance right from the start.'

Blanc listened in silence.

'The Russians took advantage of the invasion to plant a number of men amongst the refugees to the West. But that's not strictly the point, you're of interest to us for several reasons. First of all the Blunt papers in the B.M. and at the Fitzwilliam fall outside the fifty years rule. There's some legal device or other to do with trusteeship which means that they can be made available to researchers. You might, unwittingly, have stumbled on quite a lot of secret information which even now would interest the Russians. Be that as it may, there's always been the need to recruit a number of refugees for work inside Czechoslovakia. With you the difficulty is that you'd be put on trial directly you return.'

'I know that,' Blanc interrupted, 'there's a man called Busek at the Embassy who'll be seeing to it at the moment.'

'Yes, that's true,' Smith said. 'We have a man in the Embassy. If you don't leave the day after tomorrow they intend to get you out by force.'

'What can you do for me?'

'I've come with an offer. Take it or leave it. The sub-section could use you. If you accept—the visa can be extended indefinitely and could, eventually, be granted on a permanent basis. You might have to take out British nationality. But that wouldn't be for a bit. Before approaching you we've had to undertake thorough vetting procedures. Invariably with most 'candidates' there's a long waiting period. The results of the vetting, in Prague, Cambridge and London weren't known until yesterday and you're OK. There's only one problem....'

'What's that?'

'Perhaps there are two. First of all whether you'll accept the work.'

'You mean with the Foreign Office?'

'With the Foreign Office....'

'That depends on what it is.'

'That's the point. I can't tell you unless you accept in principle and practice *before* I explain it to you.'

'All right. What's the second problem?'

'Busek. Within thirty-six hours or so from now he'll be getting plans under way to have you taken to Prague. He can do this two ways. Firstly, by making a formal application for your extradition to the Home Office. This will only be successful if you haven't been granted an extension to your visa. So, if you accept our offer this can be arranged. Alternatively, they can get you by force from this flat. But here luck is on your side. You'll probably not be aware that the Czech and Russian Embassies have already kidnapped five Czech resistance workers from this country, two more from France and some two dozen from Vienna, including incidentally Magda Holotík. The very strongest protestations have been made to the Czechoslovak Foreign Ministry in Prague. Our Ambassador, along with the French and Austrian, have received assurances that it won't happen again. In fact, the French threatened to take the matter to the U.N. So you can be sure that Busek will not actually approach you. It really isn't worthwhile; particularly in view of the easing up of relations between the British and Czech governments just now. The Anglo-Czech Trade Treaty is to be signed next month and the Czechs and the Russians don't want it messed up.'

Smith's face was credible yet unsmiling. He talked with his chin tucked into his collar with a concerned frown. It sounded too good to be true, though Blanc was still unsure about Busek.

'How can you be sure that Busek won't move?'

'If he intends to we'll find out through our contact within the Embassy. At the moment Busek's trying his hardest to ensure that your application is rejected. And at the moment he reckons he's succeeded.'

'All right then Smith,' Blanc said hesitantly, 'what is it you want me to do?'

'First of all accept....'

'It seems as though I've no alternative.'

'You could say that. On the other hand it would be nicer for you if you knew you'd volunteered.'

'For God's sake, why?'

'For peace of mind.'

Blanc still had the possibility of hiding out in Vienna at the back of his mind. But if as Smith had said Magda Holotík had been taken by the Russians, he had no one there to go to, assuming Smith wasn't lying. Intuitively he felt that Smith had told the truth.

'Let's reach a compromise solution,' Smith said. 'Let's put it this way. You'll have to leave this flat and Clare have already received your letter discontinuing your grant. My sub-section at the Foreign Office will require you to be briefed fairly extensively before you take on our work. So, in other words, you'll have to get out of here.'

'What's the compromise?'

'That you leave here tomorrow night. I'll arrange a car and from then you'll be, as it were, in our care.'

'Where does it involve going to?'

'To the country.'

'What do you mean – the country?'

'We always run our briefings well out of London. It avoids confusion about security arrangements. It's generally a good idea.'

'But the compromise—you still haven't told me what it is.'

'Just that you come with me tomorrow night. And we can go from there.'

Blanc never agreed in so many words. It was just taken for granted that Smith would collect him the following night, and they would go 'to the country'. Before he left, Smith asked him about his rent agreement. It was, Blanc assured him, sewn up and finished. He asked him about his friends in London, but, Blanc explained, he didn't have any. 'Strangely enough though, someone did speak to me this morning. In the B.M.'

'Cyril Barnes,' Smith said.

'Yes. How did you know?'

'He's been one of the shadows for the past months. He's been working his way closer to you all the time.'

'He's pretty close then,' Blanc said. 'He's due here, tonight, rather he was.'

'I came instead.'

Smith left him alone again just before midnight.

The next morning the sky was limp and overcast, hanging over London in a menacing way. By the time Smith came back that night Blanc had packed a small canvas holdall and as they left Diadem Court the first heavy drops of rain fell. They spotted the pavement and collected in the dust on the piles of cardboard boxes full of refuse at the end of the alleyway.

Then the rain broke.

They ran to a low, black official-looking car parked in Wardour Street. There was an aerial on its roof, the kind that taxi drivers use giving their business a superficial air of intrigue or of high speed control. As they got into the car Blanc looked round into Diadem Court.

'I told you,' Smith said, 'Busek won't bother you. You'll be more concerned with other people from now on.'

'That, I am most grateful to you for,' Blanc said with studied fluency.

The car swept up into Oxford Street, round the park and out west of London. Blanc was in the back and from time to time he asked Smith where they were going, but Smith didn't look round and merely said something about friends and three hours.

The car began to mist up, rain ran off the windscreen and oncoming headlights glared up at them off the motorway.

As they neared Reading the driver reached under the dash-board for a small vented microphone.

'F.S. to R.McC. Reading ring road.'

The car became hotter so the driver turned on a cooling fan. The air blew up into the back between two front bucket seats. Bucket seats, thought Blanc, weren't official. He gazed out through the side windows.

It seemed illogical that Smith or the sub-section he talked about should want anything to do with him, unless some kind of blackmail was involved. Yet the Foreign Office, or Foreign Service as Smith called it, would surely keep clear of blackmail. On the other hand it was perfectly true that the Blunt papers, some of them, were still top secret and that he had been given special clearance to see them. The remaining papers were hardly of national consequence. But something in Smith's voice had indicated that they wanted him for something else, and that the Blunt papers were just a convenient pretext. The visa had forced their hands. It made them decide whether to abandon the idea of using him, or, on the other hand, to put it to good use as a recruitment incentive.

Blanc felt exhausted and, with a sense that he had given in to Smith all too easily, he resigned himself to whatever the car was taking him to: it couldn't be much worse than a trial in Prague.

Once beyond Reading the roads were entirely unknown to Blanc. A signpost flickered by, and he strained round to see it, but it was too dark once they'd passed. He listened to the continuous rushing of the wet road. Less frequently than before a car blazed towards them, dipped its lights, shook them with its windstream and was gone.

Exhausted, Blanc slept fitfully.

He had fallen sideways across the back seat when they finally stopped. Looking up he could see lights outside the car. They had pulled up next to a low farmhouse.

A plastic raincoat was pushed over the front seat towards him. He got out of the car into the rain and draped the coat over his head like a tent. The driver turned the car round and drove off along the drive from the farm. Smith led the way over the soaked cobbled courtyard and into a low kitchen.

'This is Blanc,' Smith said.

'I'm Richard McCall.' He put down a towel and shook Blanc by the hand and led them through the kitchen into a low-beamed living-room. As if telling himself about a job well done, Smith ran his hand absent-mindedly across the handle of an Aga stove.

'Have you had anything to eat?' McCall asked.

'Not since yesterday.'

'You two sit here. I'll get something.'

The room was very low. There were no pictures on the walls. A fire burned weakly in the hearth, the wet logs hissing evenly.

'Who is he exactly?' Blanc asked.

Smith lay back deep into the sofa.

'Richard McCall? He's an ex-Naval Officer who went into the Stock Exchange. He free-wheels between the Foreign Office, the Home Office and the police. Depends on what's happening. Otherwise he works on the East European Desk; arranges cultural visits, business exchanges, trade delegations, that sort of thing.' Smith leant forward and poked the fire.

McCall brought a tray of food and a glass decanter with a fine gold chain round its neck.

He watched Blanc and Smith eat.

'Where's the driver?'

'He's gone back,' Smith said.

McCall turned to Blanc. 'Cairns was your old professor in Cambridge wasn't he?'

Blanc nodded.

'He thinks a lot of you.'

McCall poured out three glasses from the decanter.

'You know his wife?'

'I met her once.'

'Marguerite's well preserved. Surprising really, when you think what a rough time she had during the war. Did you ever notice her left arm?'

Blanc recalled Cairns's wife dropping a tray of tea cakes one Sunday afternoon during a restrained tea party. Smith had been there too.

'She had it broken by the Gestapo. In seven places. They

20

used a small pointed hammer. She never said a thing,'
McCall said with approval. 'You ought to read the S.O.E. book
sometime.' He sipped at his glass and wiped off a white smear
from its rim. 'You must be rather tired by now, there's a
room here for you. Over the stables.' He leaned forward on
his chair. 'You really don't have to worry about this visa.
Our people have already arranged it and you needn't worry
about Busek either. Meanwhile, one way and another, we've
got to keep you out of trouble, which means no more work
at the B.M. for a bit.' McCall half smiled at him. 'It's all sorted
out. The main thing is that we look after you properly down
here, isn't it?' It was the sort of question you couldn't reply
to.

Smith showed him to his room across the courtyard
immediately after they finished eating. It was above some
stables at the top of a wooden staircase.

'Bathroom here. You should have all you want. There'll be
some breakfast at eight. The rain should stop by morning.'

Blanc unpacked his case and looked out over the courtyard.
The rain was still falling on the roof of the farmhouse, and
the wind was bending the trees beyond it. In the farmhouse
itself three small windows were still lit on the top floor,
filtering light through thin curtains. By pressing his face
against the window of his room, Blanc could see something
glittering on the top of the slate roof. He turned off his light
and looked out again. A black steel mast was attached to
the roof, from which several metal branches forked out. It
was too large for a television aerial, then he remembered
the radio telephone in the car. They had their own radio
telephone system.

He turned back the crisp laundered sheets. He was badly
in need of sleep.

4

The rain cleared the next morning as Smith said it would. The sky spread itself outwards and upwards and it seemed as though the petal-shaped clouds were being pulled across it. For some days the wind would hold, just at the time between summer and winter when it became noticeable that the leaves were beginning to fall. It was the time of the year that artists and poets somehow ignore, a moment between seasons which exists in its own right, whose quality is simply that of change and nothing else: so who need bother to make it permanent? It would be a lie.

Blanc crossed the courtyard and looked up at the mast. He could see that two silver wires held it against the wind, each attached to iron brackets at either end of the roof. McCall was leaving the house.

'Help yourself inside.' And he held out his hands as if to say 'It's all yours.' 'There's some cold ham and coffee. When you're ready I'd like to talk to you. We can walk on the downs.'

Blanc ate breakfast on his own. The kitchen had a permanent look, a dog basket in one corner filled with three or four ex-Naval blankets, all grey, except for some brown marks made by a hot iron. Tea towels hung from the ceiling on a wooden rack fixed at each end by a curving metal holder. The floor was paved and worn, and there were long pale streaks across the stone, as though someone had spilled bleach on it.

Blanc ate and gazed out of the window. The farmhouse was in a hollow. A stubbled cornfield revealed bare parallel lines of earth towards the top of a hillock. He played with his cup, tilting it backwards and forwards.

He tried to remember any of the conversations he had

engaged Smith in at Cambridge and any more hints of Smith's real occupation. But the more he racked his mind the more he confused himself.

He walked across to the window again.

The drive continued round the side of the hollow to the left and the trees behind it were entangled with a full undergrowth of old hedgerow and nettles. McCall interrupted his thoughts, 'Some old boots over there,' he pointed to the corner of the kitchen. 'They should fit you. Let's walk for a while. Francis is busy with the radio.'

They picked their way along one of the wet ribs of the cornfield until the farmhouse disappeared from sight behind them and headed for a long and gradual rise on which there were small dots. They looked like sheep or boulders. Until they moved it was hard to tell which.

McCall had an easy charm. 'Got any family?'

'No. Unfortunately not; my mother died four years ago so my father left Prague and went to Canada.'

'Whereabouts?'

'Montreal.'

'Is he still there?'

'No, he died there last year and the house was sold up. A firm of lawyers sent me the proceeds, not much. But it helped.'

'No one else—brothers, sisters?'

'No one.'

'No relations at all then, no one in Prague?'

'No. Though there might be some of my father's. I think he had a brother just outside but I never met him. I believe he was a doctor or something.'

'So you're on your own.'

'That's right.'

The wind took their voices away so they had to shout.

'Ever thought of marrying?'

'If the right girl turns up.'

'No,' McCall shouted, 'I mean is there anyone lined up?'

McCall held apart the strands of a barbed wire fence and let Blanc through.

'There's no one,' Blanc said.

'Do you want to go back? To Prague?'

'Of course. One day; but on my own terms.' They crossed a ditch. Its water was running a rust brown. Then the rise flattened out in front of them. McCall looked preoccupied. 'How much did Francis explain to you?'

'That he could arrange for me to get some sort of visa extension.'

'Have you ever thought of working for the Foreign Service?'

'The British one?'

'Right.'

'No. I can't say I have. I mean it'd be impossible anyway....'

'Not altogether. You haven't had time to talk about it to Francis: but it's not bad now, pay's good and better than it used to be. You'd come in at a high scale and your languages would be useful.'

'I'm a foreigner, McCall, a Czech, I may not sound it, but it's a fact.'

'It won't make any difference. Not for what we want you to do. It's only a freelance job and very temporary. It's by way of a secondment, from now.'

'From now?'

'Yes.' Blanc looked at him amazed, 'It's not exactly the Foreign Service,' McCall went on, 'it's a sub-section of it, for which both Smith and myself work. Meanwhile you'll be staying down here for briefing. Is that all right?'

'I've no alternative.'

'It's just that we like people to volunteer, Blanc, so much easier for everyone.'

'But you've been watching me for months. So Smith said anyway. Quite why you should put up this front about volunteering I can't think.'

McCall wouldn't give him a straight answer.

'People join the Foreign Service for different reasons— money, prestige, travel and so on. In your case there's no alternative.'

'You've said that already.'

'I know. But I'm implying that you'll be required to work under Foreign Service regulations.'

'All right,' Blanc said thoughtfully.

'I hope you understand. Let me put it another way: I recently visited Parkhurst to interrogate two spies and they'd been broken by the place. I can tell you, it was pretty horrible.'

'What's that supposed to mean?'

'Draw your own conclusions,' McCall said, looking at the ground.

Blanc said nothing more. The wet clotted soil stuck to his rubber boots picking up dead weeds and tiny pebbles. They walked the length of another field before reaching a hill from which they could see the farm. The view was impressive and as they looked at it a sheep bolted off down the hillside overturning some small rocks as it went. They crossed a tar road and followed the drive to the farmhouse.

'What conclusions was I supposed to draw from your remark about the spies in Parkhurst?'

'Surely, Blanc ...' McCall said with sarcasm.

'If you guessed,' Blanc said, 'that I had it in my mind to put a spoke in the wheel of your plans for me—if they turn sour; then you're pretty well right.'

'If,' McCall replied as if engaged in a dispute of logic, 'if you were really going to do that, then the first thing you'd have made sure of was that I had no inkling of it.' He paused. 'And, if I thought you would do that, tonight you'd be in Parkhurst or on your way there, certain of the fact both that you'd be handed over to Busek at the earliest opportunity and that you'd be branded as a political agent working against the interests of this country. And as Busek wouldn't know about it, he'd be doubly displeased. I'm not an alarmist, but it's just as well for us all to know where we stand right from the start.'

They walked across the courtyard. A spaniel puppy ran out to meet them and jumped around McCall's legs and then around Blanc's. His feet felt hot inside the boots. The spaniel stretched up against his trousers so he buried his fingers into the folds of its neck; the fine hair felt dry and soft. McCall flicked his fingers. 'Come on, boy, come on, come on.' The spaniel sprang up at him. 'Good boy.'

Blanc realised now that he and the little puppy shared the same master.

5

McCall dominated the farmhouse. The days were arranged round him. In the mornings he drove off early in a black saloon on his own along the road which curved around the downs. After five miles it joined the road from Hungerford to Swindon. There he went to the station to meet the train which brought his dispatches. The official papers were packed in one, sometimes two, sealed tins.

The journeys took up the whole morning but by lunchtime he would be back at the farmhouse. Then, early in the afternoon, the three men looked over the morning delivery.

For the first few days nothing made any sense to Blanc. McCall simply passed quarto sheets of typescript to Smith. The latter read them and more often as not passed them back to McCall without comment.

At the end of the first week, on a Saturday, McCall still hadn't brought Blanc in on the discussions. So Blanc asked if he could take a book to his bedroom and join them later.

He ran his finger along the bookshelves and settled on *The Great Impersonation* by E. Phillips Oppenheim. There seemed to be so little urgency about the business. A prewar thriller would fill out the time.

In his room he sprawled on his bed.

Blanc gave the impression of being thin and even fragile, if only because his face was a little haggard for a man still under thirty. It was a face which wouldn't command immediate respect from men but which nevertheless appealed to women. More than once someone had described his usual expression as contemplative. In looks Blanc was the odd man out in the trio at the farmhouse.

Now, at the point when Blanc felt he was wasting his time,

McCall directed his attention towards him. Smith woke him at nine in the evening. Blanc was surprised he had slept so long.

The three men ate dinner together and McCall was in high spirits. 'For the first time,' he said laughingly, 'I thought something had gone wrong. The sub-section sent *six* tins this morning. Now we'll bring you in.' He looked at Blanc with satisfaction.

Blanc just nodded. He still felt menaced by McCall who had all the qualities of the natural authoritarian and Blanc didn't much like them. You sensed with McCall that he managed by 'fixing' things or by having friends who could fix them for him. Smith, on the other hand, gave the impression of being ambitious but probably wasn't. He was self-contained and he kept to the regulations, whatever they were.

Both men represented a threat—of one sort of blackmail. Yet they were also his protection. Without them Blanc could have walked the 10 miles to Swindon, caught a train to Paddington. After that he would be free, though of course there was still Busek. He felt that the freer he allowed himself to be the more the others would confine him.

After dinner the table was pushed to the wall. McCall sifted through the papers. 'All of them are marked,' he said, holding up a closely typed memorandum for Blanc to look at. 'Most of them have classifications. Here's one *Addressee's Eyes Only*. Mine. They're also signed by the people who've seen them at the sub-section. *General Officer*, he's the overall head of the division to which we belong; the *Duty Officer, Typists, Despatch Officer*. These are the only people who've seen them.'

'The red number,' Smith interrupted, 'is the Microfilm Reference.'

'We'll talk about these in a minute,' McCall said. There was a regular beeping from the room above. McCall pointed a finger at the ceiling and Smith got up to see to the noise from the radio room.

As he left he picked up a file with a precise, almost snappy movement at odds with the largeness of his features.

Nothing seemed to be shared between him and McCall, except the sense that each knew the other's place. There was no obvious interpretation to be offered for the way McCall looked up at Smith as he shut the door. Blanc realised that 'friends' were not 'friends' in the accepted sense, rather they were people dedicated to the same ends. It stopped there.

McCall had an incisive mind and spoke with a fluency which comes easily to someone who has worked on one problem for months without interruption. Only rarely would he break off, as if thinking of something else. He was used to fitting facts together and forming arguments from them, and then, with surprising speed, drawing conclusions which he would number, 'There are four points then ...'

Eventually, without admitting that he was speculating, he arrived at what he called his 'solution' or an indication of where it might lie if *all* the facts were available.

When Smith shut the door after him, McCall began, for the first time, to talk about himself. If he couldn't reassure Blanc about his predicament, then personal reminiscences might help, as personal as appropriate. It seemed that his present work obsessed him. It was as though his whole life had led up to it, and that now at last he was about to reach beyond himself to spectacular success.

'I'm not sure a serviceman should be reflective; it diminishes confidence I think. One needs an ordered pattern of thought. I never grasped that at Cambridge, not until after I was transferred from the Navy to Special Operations Executive. That's where Cairns and I got to know each other. They sent me to Vichy to get the communists out of the last strongholds, then the Gaullists took over, so I came back.'

Blanc watched McCall's face. The fine pores of his skin were prickled with closely shaved stubble. It was a drab, almost blue complexion.

'Some of the S.O.E. people transferred into the Foreign Service at the end of the war. There were a lot of people on the fringes, most of them divorced—an occupational hazard. Smith was one of them, a fringe man, and divorced too. Things have a way of linking up, don't you think? There are only so many London clubs you can join, that's the reason we got onto the Royal Services Club—where you start work. It's pleasant enough, a bit dull perhaps, but safe.'

McCall pulled out a folded sheet of paper from the file on his lap.

'This is the layout of the place, the original architect's plan.' He handed it to Blanc. 'You'll need to know it. Look at the passageways, kitchens, approach to the cellars. Look at them carefully. Eventually you'll get to know it all without thinking. Remember the cellars.'

He spread out more papers on the sofa.

'Your money's looked after, the budget's been stretched: we've got a hefty sum for you. More of that later. You'll be responsible to myself, Smith and Helmsman. There's no bureaucracy involved, no letters, nothing written. Nothing is to be put on paper. You'll meet Helmsman at the club, when you get there.'

'Who is Helmsman?'

'I said you'll meet when you get there.' McCall sifted through the papers again and bent them back at the top left hand corners when he had finished with them.

'So what do I do once I get to the club?' Blanc asked.

'It's to do with *listening*. That's all. You'll be given several sophisticated hearing devices. Helmsman will tell you what to do with them. They'll be planted on or about several people.'

'Who?'

'I'll come to that.'

'What about this club, about membership?'

'It's been applied for. It'll be through within the week.'

'*Who* exactly are the devices intended for?'

'You'll be told. All in good time,' McCall said stiffly. 'But there's one thing,' he added, 'should you be caught placing them or for that matter interrupted in anything else by those we're interested in, don't expect any assistance from me or the sub-section. You won't get it. You're on your own once you're caught. There's no reason why you shouldn't be successful and if you are there's the visa to think of, the—let's call it the negation of Busek, and a cash payment.'

'How much?'

'It's usually several thousand. I wouldn't quarrel with it.

It's more than you'd see in a lifetime in Prague. I wouldn't quarrel.'

'I can't very well, not with blackmail.'

'No one said it was.'

'That's what it amounts to though.'

'You can call it what you like.' McCall's expression revealed nothing. It was bland, almost curious. The morality of it didn't seem to affect him. McCall shifted again in his chair. Blanc wanted to break into his thoughts, to solicit what he was being asked to do.

'You're not really telling me that I'm to poke around with some gadgets for six months.'

'That's one way of putting it.'

'Do you mean to say that you've no idea *what* you're listening for.'

'Half true. It's more complex than that. There are four men who've been watched by us for several years. Their names are linked in several ways. It's possible to trace security leaks to them; largely through acquaintances, some illegal arms deals, the harbouring of weapons and extreme right wing politics.'

McCall was choosing his words carefully. He was giving Blanc just enough, not too much; just the vaguest picture.

'It's full of intricacies. When the socialists came in they made extensive cuts in the allocation to the Security Services, to all the various branches. In fact, I think the whole reduction amounts to the equivalent of the cost of financing a large percentage of the embassies in Europe. But don't imagine that we're involved in some sort of *espionage* work. I don't want to hear the word spy.'

'That's what it sounds like to me.'

'You're mistaken.' He was sorting his ideas out on his fingers. He had been through it before, the evenness of his voice showed it. 'No one can afford to run a large permanent staff which feeds the agents; the risks are too great. The same goes for keeping minor embassy officials watching out for defectors, potential or otherwise. There may be a few scattered around, but the methods have changed, so have the people, and the Cold War itself.'

It was all rehearsed. It made sense.

'A government has to be *seen* to have a security service of some sort,' McCall said with conviction, 'presumably it makes the voters feel safe.' He laughed. 'It's basically a risk all the same. The game goes on at a very sophisticated level.' 'Call it what you like,' Blanc said, almost to himself. 'But it's spying.' 'No.' McCall chewed on his teeth. 'It operates on a short term basis. Not on the long term, that's what used to happen. That was spying. Now the whole business works like a jigsaw. But, it's never put together. No one, like no one person, knows the solution. There's no picture on the box.'

Even before he said it, Blanc knew he would sound a sceptic—'Why bother at all?'

'Simply because the bits exist. Everyone goes on making a constant effort to fit them together.'

'What are they then?'

'The valuable information is scientific, technological and political; some of it's useful to unfriendly countries. Some isn't. Space research information isn't. But anything which would embarrass a major political figure is. Even an assassination plot.'

'Is that *political?*'

'Of course. Then there's information on the research by-products. That's of marginal use. Then again information on technical *innovation* isn't because it can't be kept secret for long. And anyway the expense of that sort of secrecy is too great. But that it should be kept secret for at least a year is crucial. The same goes for certain sorts of conspiracy— the kind we're dealing with.'

Blanc sat up.

McCall continued, 'However, a bureaucratic organisation built up to see to this would have security risks. Parkinson's Law in these setups is the rule rather than the exception.'

McCall paused briefly.

'We employ officers, they used to be called agents. After vetting they're employed for short periods. They are disposable assets and can't be used twice. Anyway the jigsaw is constantly in motion and exists on many levels.' Blanc nodded as if to say go on; McCall didn't need any asking.

'The operation works on *Need To Know*. That's not a new

idea but it's been developed more than before. Each officer knows only a part of the total picture. Just a few bits of the jig-saw. I can't go into it any more. Except that it's been in operation since Philby. And his danger, at least the threat of it, has been defused. I suppose it could happen again, but no one can predict how. After Philby an entirely new system of computerised vetting was introduced. It works extremely well. Its codes are programmed at three different centres. One in Washington by the Central Intelligence Agency. Another outside London. And a third by the U.S. Systems Intelligence Agency in Colorado. They work on a sort of interlocking basis and so, when it comes to it, no one person knows how the interlocking of information takes place. It's impossible for anyone to break the codes unless they have prior knowledge of all the programmes being fed into all three computers. So, Philby, like the fictional heroes and others he inspired, was part of an intelligence hierarchy which has been completely dissolved....'

McCall broke off as Smith called from the stairs.

'It's for you. I've said you'll take it now....'

'I'll come.'

McCall looked at Blanc. 'It won't take a minute.'

On his own Blanc imagined the guardians of this concept of security shuffling along corridors of hard shiny tiles like robots. The air-conditioned corridors would be just too cold and just too brightly lit. A human, understandable secret was potent: the quiet deceit of a mistress, a flight from the ordinary. His own intrusion into someone else's marriage.

He thought of the one girl he had enjoyed in England—it had only happened once.

There had been a controlled outbidding of a tall, strongly built girl in a Cambridge auction room.

'Two pounds ten, fifteen. *Three*. Three pounds, three five, ten, fifteen. Four, four pounds, at four pounds. At four pounds. At four pounds. At four pounds five, ten, fifteen. *Five*. Five five, ten, fifteen. At six. At six. At six pounds. *Clack*. The name?'

'Blanc.'

And he had bought a milking stool at about six times its worth.

She had walked across to him, twenty-five with thick and soft blond hair falling down around her face. She was eye-stopping with a wide mouth and smile. She had rubbed her hair away from her eyes with the back of her hand.

'What on *earth* do you want that for?'

She laughed with an infectious gaiety.

'Where do you live?'

And one Sunday, Blanc couldn't remember the date, she had walked into his room and they made love. She had kissed his neck like a cat licking its offspring. Then, it may have been in May, she told him 'they' were going to Sweden. And she left. Blanc had once seen her husband's name in a U.N.E.S.C.O. publication, above an article on Scandinavian mythology.

A year later he thought he saw her in Russell Square. He wasn't sure. It was the first time a very beautiful girl had, in so many words, picked him up.

He remembered too that she had said he looked more Slav than Czech.

'You've got wild eyes.' she said.

Blanc had found it rather funny. And he was still smiling to himself when McCall returned with the files which he had carefully taken with him.

He sat down.

'The four men,' he announced, and there was a trace, a suggestion of reluctance in his voice. 'Let's look at them.'

Once again he sifted through the papers.

'Bear in mind that they all fit together. That they have, as it were, reached the last stages of their particular jigsaw. The difference is ...' He paused. 'It involves assassination....'

'I see,' said Blanc, with unexpected anger. 'You didn't tell me....'

'Hold on, you're not hired to kill anyone. And as we've no idea who *they* intend to kill you needn't worry. And it's no concern of yours *how* our operation is to be organised, neither is it your affair if anything goes wrong.' His voice was low. 'There's no reason why your part should go wrong. You do what you're told. We'll look at their backgrounds. Briefly.'

He took his time. McCall read from the files. From time to time he looked up at Blanc to elaborate on details.

Charles Donnelly had been born in Malton in Yorkshire. His father had been a wool merchant and had sent his son to a public school in the north of England. There he had achieved conventional success. Blanc asked what that meant.

'He played in the Rugby Football team. Won a cup for High Jumping.'

Blanc found it amusing.

'Then Donnelly joined the Rifle Brigade at the outbreak of war and had an undistinguished war record. Except that he had been mentioned in despatches.'

'In what?'

'A medal. He got a medal. Rather not quite.' McCall was irritated.

'He finished the war as a major and was a transport officer in occupied Berlin. In 1955 he was sent as Military Attaché to Helsinki and two years later retired as a Colonel. He married a Finnish girl but she disliked England and left him. That was shortly after their return from Helsinki. They've no children and now Donnelly lives alone in Twickenham. He still visits Helsinki twice a year for the company he works for—Kent Home Suppliers Limited. Even as an attaché he came under the scrutiny of the security man in the Embassy as a result of his meetings with a Danish journalist called Skovgaard who has a record for illegal arms dealing. Otherwise Donnelly's immensely respectable—a member of the M.C.C. as well as the Royal Services Club in St James's Square.'

The second file that McCall read from was devoted to Clifford Margot, solicitor, born in 1917, educated at St Edward's School, Oxford and Christ Church. He was a recognised expert on company law, and once briefly married. He had been captured by the Germans during the war, had escaped

34

to France and disguised himself as an undertaker in Angers. His father had been a wealthy Paris industrialist and his mother who lived to the age of eighty-five was Russian by birth. He had been very attached to his mother. He had numerous family connexions in the Loire and in Paris. That was one of the reasons he'd been sent to Angers. He was now a consultant to an electronics company with extensive contracts for supplies to the U.S. Navy. He travelled regularly to Paris and less frequently to Bonn, Frankfurt and Washington.

He was, as it happened, an acknowledged expert on caving and in 1959 had published *Survival and Escape in Cave Exploration* which had gone into three editions and was still regarded as a standard work.

In 1963 he was chosen, under the Macmillan government, to serve on a Sub-Committee of the Standing Security Commission. (His appointment was much criticised by some but otherwise had been overlooked and he had not been vetted.) He lived alone in Hampstead and was a member of the Royal Services Club.

The third file described Donald Ames, the vicar of St Margaret's, Kensington. He had had a dubious career in right-wing politics just before the war and his name had, even until recently, been associated with The Link. He was an amateur archaeologist of repute and had been badly shaken by his wife's adultery with a member of the Westminster Archaeological Society some five years ago. He had been a member of the Society since the year of its founding in 1949. His particular contribution to it had been a number of erudite papers on sewerage networks in Regents Park and under the West End of London. Since 1952 he had been a member of the Royal Services Club.

The fourth file described Dennis Waterman, a fifty-year-old bachelor who had inherited a considerable fortune of some two hundred thousand pounds from an aunt in South Africa when she died in the late 1950's. She had owned a diamond mine.

His uncle, who died in 1963, had served the last senile

ten years of his life on the executive committee of the Royal Services Club. Waterman, naturally, was a member and knew all the others well. He had been a senior research worker at the Royal Botanical Gardens at Kew for some years (there was some doubt as to when he was taken on full time, mainly because he had worked there unpaid for a few years). Waterman had developed a system of automatic greenhouse ventilation. This controlled the ventilators in the roof of greenhouses with cylinders of mineral oil. As the temperature rose so the oil expanded and drove a piston which opened the ventilators. Although the system was not in itself new, Waterman had found a unique combination of oils which were extraordinarily sensitive to temperature change. He was also a licensed pilot and lived in a Keeper's Lodge within his account.

McCall then handed some other papers to Blanc. One looked like a balance sheet and was an analysis of each man's bank account since 1955. They revealed very little. Except that considerable sums of money had been paid in to each man's account from an unidentified source in 1965, '66, '67 and '68. All of them had made successful investments except Margot, who had already drawn most of his money from his account.

There seemed to be no other pattern common to all four men. Each of them was respectable in his way, some of them experts, each had received the payments, all of them were members of the same London men's club.

'Their backgrounds are what we'd call all right,' said McCall, 'on the outside. We know the payments have come from an East German agent. We think they are part of advance payments, the rest to be paid "on delivery".'

Blanc looked at the descriptions again. They were all roughly the same age. And, as McCall had said, all of them *were* conventional—up to a point.

'What do you make of them?' McCall asked.

'Not much more than is here. Donnelly and Margot are what you call professional men.'

Blanc smiled. 'In the contradictory English sense.'

'Which is?'

'Indefinable, respectable, but money earning. Normally the two qualifications would be in opposition—at least if the emphasis is on money.'

McCall laughed. 'I wouldn't have thought you'd have known as much about the English.'

'Maybe not,' said Blanc.

'And what else?'

'I suppose they're reliable. As the prayer puts it—"of good report". I imagine they aren't the subject of too many rumours. Liked by everyone. Modest. Popular. Kind. But only because everyone says so.'

'And what do you infer from that? That they're harmless.'

'Not at all. The Englishman always prefers his reports secondhand. "Ask so and so, he'll tell you." Cairns once told me at Clare that it didn't matter what he wrote in an undergraduate's report, but what he *didn't* write. It's not what's in them that counts, it's what *isn't*.'

'That's roughly what we've got hold of you for,' McCall said.

'To tell you what's not in here?' Blanc pointed at the files.

'That's it.'

'And how the hell do you expect me to find out?'

'It won't be too difficult.'

'You haven't answered my question.'

'I will do. Soon enough.'

'We believe,' McCall said ponderously, 'in meeting force with force, or rather kind with kind. And you look right to be the background listener in the club. Maybe elsewhere too.'

'That doesn't get me anywhere. Who *exactly* are the four men? Who do they work for?'

'It's on the files. At least the background material is. Here's something else.'

McCall read from another photocopied paper.

'This is a doctor's analysis.'

'A what?'

'A report from the doctor. It's policy to get them. We've got the one only. On Margot. From his psychiatrist. There's some sort of sex problem.'

McCall hesitated.

'There's an early history of homosexuality.'

'But you said he'd been married.'

37

'Precisely.'

'Well?'

'That's why his wife left him.'

'Tell me more.'

'In good time.'

Thank God, thought Blanc, that they didn't have doctor's reports on him. Though he didn't think that he had a sex problem.

'It all fits together,' McCall said. 'We'll take it slowly for the moment. You'll get to know all you need to as it goes along.'

The rest of that evening they continued to discuss Donnelly, Margot, Waterman and Ames: their families, friends, time spent at the Royal Services Club, their varying political sympathies.

Smith joined them and they talked about the Royal Services Club—how easy Helmsman had found it to get accepted.

'But *who* is Helmsman?' Blanc asked again.

'Helmsman will make contact with you once you get there,' McCall answered finally.

'It's all quite simple,' Smith said, reassuringly.

Blanc felt differently. And not for the last time.

The routine in the farmhouse remained unchanged.

Still McCall left each morning for the station. Once he was late and said that he'd met the vicar. Smith smiled knowingly and Blanc thought it odd that McCall should have religious sympathies. He didn't seem the type.

The radio was used less frequently. 'It's a regulation issue,' Smith said.

Blanc began to get swept up in the work. There was nothing else to do.

McCall's visits to the vicar became more frequent and Blanc noticed that when McCall offered apologies Smith would look at the older man's eyes. They flickered. One morning McCall appeared at breakfast with his eyes puffed.

Blanc thought nothing of it until much later.

On another Saturday morning, at the end of the fourth week which had dragged, McCall announced that he had an invitation to spend the night with family friends beyond Oxford, somewhere near Bicester. Blanc was asked to entertain himself: to read another Oppenheim or go to the cinema in Swindon.

Smith was going too. They would be back for lunch the next day. The radio would be shut down and the telephone could be left unanswered.

'Can you ride a B.S.A.?' McCall asked.

'A what?' Blanc said with surprise.

'A motor bike. A B.S.A.'

'Yes. As a matter of fact I can.'

'Have you got a licence?'

'No.'

'Well there's a B.S.A. in the garage. You can use it but don't kill yourself. In fact, make bloody sure you don't.'

6

Blanc was left alone.

He decided to take the bike into Swindon as McCall had suggested.

He also decided to look at the radio room. It was above the main room in the farmhouse. But it was firmly locked, so was the door to McCall's bedroom, so was Smith's.

He tried the radio room door again. No good. He looked at the clock next to the door handle.

Then he looked closer.

Stretched from the handle to the door frame was a fine hair, or it had been before he tried the door. Now it was broken. Blanc could see that it had been attached by two small dabs of glue.

McCall was hoping to find out how curious Blanc was. It seemed an unnecessary precaution. But the hair was broken. Blanc held it in his hand. It was a dark hair. Probably McCall's.

Blanc would try McCall. He pulled one of his own hairs from the top of his head. The two tiny dabs of glue were hard on the outside but were still slightly sticky on the inside. Bending down Blanc replaced the broken hair with one of his own.

He went downstairs.

The silence was oppressive. As he closed the door to the farmhouse the spaniel started to bark.

'All right boy, all right.' Blanc said soothingly.

A dried coconut shell was swinging in the wind, clattering lightly against the side of the house.

The bolt to the garage door came up easily out of its slot in between the paving stones. One of the doors was caught in the wind and slammed against the garage wall. Blanc cursed it.

The B.S.A. was leaning uncovered against the far wall. It looked powerful. Blanc pulled his jacket across him and did up all its buttons. He took down a black crash helmet from a hook and adjusted it to fit.

He wheeled the machine out into the courtyard and sitting astride it he kicked the starter. Nothing happened and he caught his ankle against part of the engine. He kicked again. And once more. The engine roared into life, filling the courtyard with its blast. He revved down, the bike jerked forward jolting his head against his neck. Then he settled down and cruised out along the track. It was uneven, and he had half a mile to cover before he reached the road. Twice he got caught in car ruts and nearly fell off. Water splashed against his trousers and soaked his shoes.

Once on the B road he turned right. From there on it would be easier.

He got up speed on the longer curves of the road and the wind went straight through his jacket, tingling his chest. The slow rise of the hills was just right and from the highest of them he could see far out towards the West. He changed up through the gears. More drive. The machine took over, so he bent lower and let rip.

His exhilaration was complete. The wind, the thrust, the graceful curving road. He forgot the claustrophobia of the farmhouse.

Swindon had once been an industrial boom town. Its railway complexes had been impressive and it remained, even now, a rail link with the West of England.

People changed trains at Swindon.

But the manufacture of the great steam engines had finished. The industrial yards and steel girdered sheds were empty and ready for demolition. They were memories talked about in the fuggy public bars. Men with greaselined faces recalled the furnaces, coal heaps, grease and sweat with respect and affection. Swindon had been warm and dark in the sheds. Now it was tall, glass and concrete. A 'very well designed town' some architect had called it. It had become enervated and public, belonging to everyone and no one.

The dark mornings were lit electrically. The gas and coal

had gone, allowing the new people to look new and clean like their work.

The people on Saturday overtime were walking briskly through the housing estates in bright pastel clothes. The boiler suits had been replaced by white coats because the men were operatives and not workers. Even the school buildings had lost the trappings of the industrial era. Now they were bright and the school bells were electric. The clangs and echoes of the pre-war classrooms had been lost in clear corridors.

The crispness was infectious and Blanc handled the motor bike with confidence as he reached the ring road. Farther on cars were turning off into parking lots alongside the football stadium and brightly scarved queues hugged its perimeter. They chanted, or they talked in small huddles; the men waving at faces they knew, raising their arms above their heads in anticipation of victory like prizefighters. Or they pushed out their arms with thumbs up.

Blanc joined the lane of traffic turning off, and headed for the centre of the town.

He left the motor bike in a car park behind a red and grey building that looked like the Town Hall. This part of the town was virtually empty but outside a cinema a group of children were kicking a half inflated football against a wall.

Two small girls watched and began prodding each other in the chest, giggling and shrieking.

Blanc bought himself a ticket for a film. There were very few other customers for the early afternoon performance, a full colour American romance ...

A girl student at the edge of a lake with her mid-western professor filled the screen. She was dangling painted toenails in the water. Her bleached jeans had been cut off just above the knee and the professor's jacket was over her shoulder.

A bent old man was hunched up two rows in front of Blanc and coughed. He sounded as if he couldn't stop. The seats began to fill up. Three women of indeterminate age in heavy coats with cotton scarves over their heads rustled their holdalls noisily. The film was self conscious ...

The young professor was talking to someone he called doctor with deferential politeness. 'It's just a loan...' The professor and the student kissed. He held her chin in his hand and toyed knowingly with the front of her check shirt.

Blanc noticed three girls, peering across the seats. One of them pointed to the row in front with her handbag, the other two pulled her into Blanc's row and along to his seat. She looked about eighteen and the way she flicked her hair back as she sat down reminded Blanc of the don's wife.

Her profile was striking, short straight nose, a full mouth slightly apart and very long blond, perhaps red hair which fell well below her shoulders.

She felt very close to him.

When their glances met Blanc started. He felt a short shock of pleasurable embarrassment. The girl didn't—she looked straight into his face without blinking.

Blanc looked away. But he could feel her eyes on him, and by looking at the bottom right of the screen he could tell she was still looking at him...

The girl student was lying on her bed, face downwards. She sobbed and her bottom lip shook against the pillow. The camera panned from her urchin cut hair to photos of her parents, a fat man with one of his arms round her and the other on the shoulder of an even fatter wife in a large flowered hat. Then the camera took in college pennants and a long flat American football.

The girl in the next seat was looking at Blanc once more. Now she offered a silent excuse by scratching her neck. So Blanc stared back. Her eyes widened.

Sometime later she let her coat, a dark fur bundle, fall to the ground. Blanc bent forwards to pick it up, she did the same and leaned close to his face.

'Six. Outside The Lawn. At six.'

She smiled as she settled in her seat again, spreading the coat across her knees....

The movie dragged on: a long funeral scene—the professor

had suffered from a blood disease. This was explained to the girl student in a sanitorium—and she was pregnant.

Blanc left the cinema. And the three girls, including the one in the fur coat, left by another exit.

It was about five. An early autumn mist blurred the street lights. Blanc walked to the car park.

The Lawn must be a pub. Or a park maybe.

He walked past the Town Hall again. There was someone to ask.

'I'm sorry,' Blanc called out. He waved apologetically at a figure in a beret crossing the front of the building. 'Excuse me, can you tell me where The Lawn is?'

'What?' the man said.

'The Lawn.'

They were standing in the shadows.

'The Lawn,' Blanc said again. 'I'm looking for ...'

'You can't miss it,' the man said briskly. 'It's a seventeenth-century manor house. Richard Jefferies' house.'

'Who's he?'

'He *was* a naturalist. Jefferies the naturalist. Haven't you heard of him?'

'No.'

The man undid the top of his coat. Blanc could see he was a vicar. He told Blanc the way.

'Thanks,' Blanc said. But the vicar was already backing away as if he were leaving the altar front, paying a sign of respect. It was a highly practised gesture. The fingertips stroked, the neck slightly bowed.

Then he turned away. 'Thanks,' Blanc called after him. The vicar didn't seem to hear.

Blanc drove the motor bike hard up the hill which led through the older, Victorian part of Swindon. Curtains had been drawn across living-room windows. A newsagent unhooked his rack of newspapers, looking like small paper masts, and one of the papers fell off and was caught by the wind blowing the pages apart and across the road.

Blanc propped his machine up against the railings of The Lawn and waited.

She was walking towards him, her fur coat undone and flapping. She couldn't be more than eighteen.

'Is that yours?' she nodded towards the motor bike.

'Yes. Do you like it?'

'It's not bad. Give me a ride.'

'O.K.' Blanc said. 'Where to?'

'Just out of the town, a short way, out on the Hungerford Road. Somewhere out there. You choose.'

They drove off, her knees tight against Blanc's thighs. He could feel her chin pressing against his back.

'Take the right one,' she shouted.

The motor bike had a powerful headlight. It picked out the cats-eyes flashing and then flickering out in the middle of the road.

'What's your name?' Blanc shouted out.

'Jean. What's yours?'

'O.B.'

'What?'

'O.B.'

'Is that all?'

'It's a sort of nickname.'

A few miles out of the town she prodded him in the back with her chin.

'Do you want to go for a walk?' she asked.

'All right. Here?'

They were half-way along a stretch of straight road, which ran a mile through thick woods either side. Blanc pulled off the road into a layby. They sat astride the motor bike.

'There's nowhere to walk here,' he said.

'Can't you take me somewhere, to talk; to your house or somewhere?' she asked.

'I don't have a house. I'm staying with some friends, temporarily, just for a few weeks, maybe longer.'

'Don't you work then?'

'No, I'm writing a book.'

'Isn't that work, I mean don't you *earn* anything?'

'Yes, it's work but I don't get much for it.'

'Are you married?' She looked at him with her head on one side.

45

'You're too young to be asking so many questions. It gives your age away.'

'Why shouldn't I ask ...?'

'I've told you. Because it gives your age away.'

She shook her head, pushed her hair away from her face and then it fell back again. 'You're stupid.'

The headlight from the motor bike beamed along the road, falling in a long and spreading patch of light in front of them.

Blanc smiled at her. 'Come back to my place for a while. I'll give you something to eat.'

She looked down at the road and pulled her coat tight across her.

'Won't there be someone there? Your friends ...?'

'No.'

'You'll take me back afterwards?'

'Yes. I'll take you back.'

The courtyard was empty, just as Blanc had expected. He let the engine roar out and then switched it off.

'It's terrific, isn't it,' the girl said.

She sat in the kitchen watching Blanc fry eggs. Yes, she was eighteen, she would leave her job in the summer and would go to art school. No, she hadn't heard of Klimt. Her father was a stock clerk and her mother a school cleaner, there were just the three of them. Yes, she was a bit old still to be at home.

Eventually she took off her fur coat. Yes, she had just bought it. She'd saved and anyway it was in a summer sale.

She stood behind Blanc looking over his shoulder and once more pressed her chin against the back of his neck, 'You don't say much, do you?' She put her arm round his waist and pressed herself up against him. 'Leave those,' she said, looking at the frying pan, 'I don't like eggs.'

She pulled him round, and Blanc let her kiss him fully.

He stared at her, 'Where did you learn to kiss like that?'

'It's natural, isn't it?'

'Yes, it's natural....'

'Well? What's wrong with that?'

'Nothing at all.'

'Didn't you enjoy it then?'

46

'Yes, I enjoyed it.'

'Come on then.' She mocked him.

Blanc knelt on the sofa, she reached up with one hand and put her finger in his mouth.

'Come on kiss me again, it's better the second time.'

She rubbed her mouth hard against his.

'Take your jacket off.'

Leaning over against the back of the sofa Blanc undressed.

'You'll get yourself into trouble one day, Jean.'

'Well, it might as well be now, mightn't it? Go on, hurry up.'

Blanc drew the curtains and turned off the light.

'Come on dear,' she said, 'a man your age too; not very demanding are you?'

She smelt faintly of cheap soap and strained her neck up towards him pushing her head down into the cushions of the sofa.

Later in the night the cold woke them both. She clacked her teeth, 'Isn't there a fire in here, it's a horrible place.'

'My room's over the stables. We'll go there.'

'No, you'd better take me home. What's the time?'

'It's about three.'

'You must take me back, they'll be mad at me.'

'You might as well stay now.'

Her eyes were puffed from sleep, her lower lip jutted forward and she yawned throwing up her hands like an uncoordinated baby.

'Come on then,' she said '... take me somewhere warm.'

She lay on her back in Blanc's bed, the sheet pulled up over her knees and her hands clasped in front. She could hear Blanc cleaning his teeth and she asked him more questions. So he told her again that he was staying with friends, they were away for the weekend. They were all working on a book about Irish history. They'd all go back to London when it was finished. 'But you can't write history,' she said. 'History either was or it wasn't, why bother to write it.' Blanc came back into the room and got into the bed beside her. He looked at her and she smiled prissily. He said: 'You should do something else on Saturdays, demonstrate or something, against the exploitation of the people on the estates, the herding of them into the factories, the tyranny of checking in and clocking out.'

'It doesn't worry me.'

'It will do soon enough.'

'I'm not worried. I can do as I want. There are plenty of boys I can have, but it's hard to know where to do it. That's why I like older men.'

'Do you know, Jean, do you know what a tart is?'

'I'm not a tart,' and suddenly she broke into tears. 'You're the one who took me, it's your fault. I'm going ...' She threw back the sheet and got out of the bed.

'You won't get far like that. Come on here, get back in the bed.'

She glared at him, and then she sobbed again. Blanc reached out and pulled her back towards him.

'I haven't said anything about you going. Stay till morning Jean. Go on. That's if your Dad hasn't sent the police out to get you first.'

'Do you think he would?'

'You know him better than I do.'

She was falling asleep against him.

The love making and her tears had taken the make up from her face. She looked her age. She couldn't have been eighteen. She was sixteen maybe, not much older. She thought only of her body and her Dad. Blanc wondered what would happen to both of them when she grew up. Her parents wouldn't care.

Occasionally she shifted in her sleep. Eventually she rolled over to the other side of the bed.

Blanc lay back with his hands behind his head and watched the dark shadows of the trees through the window.

He thought of Donnelly, Margot, Ames and Waterman. His mind raced. And he wished he could wake this girl and tell her. Just let it pour out.

She was too young for that. And too young to be in bed with him. He couldn't be sure.

She sighed in her sleep and twisted herself deeper beneath the bedclothes.

Even if the girl had been old enough nothing would have

48

been achieved by telling her. She couldn't understand. And she wouldn't understand, particularly the day the police would accompany the passport men towards him. An incorrect detail. The fast trial. He began to sweat and turned on his side uncomfortably. Hearing devices.

Blanc remembered the endless reports in *Rudé Pravo* in 1960: the hearing device in the Grand Seal of the United States which Henry Cabot Lodge revealed to the United Nations. The Russians. How typical, they couldn't restrain themselves from a symbolic gesture. Then he remembered that the accounts had been in copies of *The Times* which had been smuggled through to Prague.

Involuntarily he held Jean's hand tightly. She bit her nails. He felt them pared down to the fingertips. She was sleeping with her mouth open.

'You're human,' McCall had said. 'You may have bad luck. Something may go wrong. Don't cultivate an imagination.'

Blanc simply could not sleep.

They reheated the eggs next morning.

The motor bike started first time and Blanc took Jean very fast along the road to Swindon.

He dropped her at the outskirts.

'Can you walk from here, Jean?' he shouted above the engine. 'I must get back.'

'Yes,' she said sadly.

He kissed her on the mouth.

'You're very young Jean. And very beautiful.'

Her cheeks were still red from the ride. The autumn Sunday morning, hard and brittle in the air, had brought tears to the edges of her eyes.

'Very beautiful,' he said again.

'Will you know where to find me?' she asked.

'What's the address?'

'Remember. 8 Queen's West Estate. Write to me. I could come to London.'

'I'll write,' Blanc said.

She smiled, or tried to because this time the tears were not from the cold.

'Don't cry,' was all he could think of to say. It hurt him to see her like this.

She stood waving at the motor bike until it disappeared. The roads on the downs were wet with the melting frost.

'Hope you've missed us,' McCall was standing in the doorway of the farmhouse when Blanc returned.

'It's a fine machine,' Blanc said.

McCall was pulling on some rubber boots. 'I'm getting some exercise,' he said airily. 'Did you have a good time?'

'Fine, thanks.'

'Get some lunch then. We can go on when I get back.'

Blanc was pleased to let Smith talk on over lunch.

'How did you get on with Cairns at Cambridge?' Smith asked him.

'Well enough.'

'Richard likes him a great deal. They're two of a kind—distant, somewhat too masculine. That's why Cairns never got a desk in London.'

'He worked for you as well?'

'From time to time. On recruitment. That meant he didn't have to be desk bound. The sub-section goes for intuition, they have to. Sensibilities to match the computers. Cairns never had to embroil himself in inter-departmental rivalry. So he avoided the trap of icy memos beloved of the desk bound.'

Blanc wasn't listening. He thought of Jean, of the four men, of Busek.

'All that's gone,' Smith said with contentment. 'They just bitch about the computers, the General Officer and the empire builders. They whine. Cairns wouldn't have fitted. Neither does Richard really. Except they can't do without him.'

'And you ...'

Smith didn't get the point. 'Me? I transferred from the Foreign Service. Went to the Embassy in Oslo at the time of the Russian tests in the Arctic. We hung around the north of Norway. Ski trails vanishing over the border, very romantic stuff. Then the year at Cambridge on Russian. After that they gave me a desk in Soviet Counter

Intelligence, it's a big outfit now. Then I joined Richard on this thing.'

'What's the conspiracy?' Blanc asked directly.

'We don't know. Yet. That's what we hope you and Helmsman will discover for us.'

'Who is Helmsman?' Blanc insisted.

'Damn fine, very bright. You'll meet soon enough.'

Blanc gave up. Smith spoke with an earnestness which suggested he was in league with his listener. It was a confidential tone, without the paternal quality of a priest who speaks as though some great cathedral may amplify the confessional mumblings in a nightmare of indiscretion. It was the pitch of voice which stamped the sons of service officers living in depleted circumstances. Blanc had met plenty of them at Cambridge. It served to stop further questions.

When it came to the last of the briefings, McCall looked very tired. Smith was inscrutable and Blanc was apprehensive.

Time was running out.

McCall spread out his files. They went over Donnelly again, the usual times he visited the Royal Services Club, his relations with the other three. Donnelly was recognisable by his smoothed-down hair. And his well-fed look.

Margot had what McCall called 'a dark unpleasant sort of face'. That could mean almost anything. There was only one blurred photograph of Margot in his house at the end of a long and mature garden, and a dated photo of Donnelly's Finnish in-laws—the sort of photograph which derives from the poses of sporting teams—the old and the tall at the back, the young and small at the front. A few people were sitting with knees crossed at either side.

The information was endless and to Blanc much of it was meaningless. Only Waterman still seemed to lead a very unusual life, particularly for a man who worked with green-houses. He would disappear for long periods at a time. He was a law unto himself at Kew Gardens and no one seemed to mind. There were over fifty reports from Embassies throughout Europe. He had been seen in places as different

51

as a striptease club in Vienna and a private garden in Paris. There were no photographs of him.

In spite of their immaculate compilation, the files conveyed to Blanc no more than newspaper obituaries might have done.

Two days before he was to leave for London, McCall, Blanc and Smith went out onto the downs for the last walk with the dog.

'You haven't asked many questions?' McCall said to Blanc casually.

'On the contrary. I'm not sure which ones to ask.'

'Remember that you'll be dealing with *professional* men each with a wide circle of influential friends.'

'I gathered that.'

'Worth remembering though.'

'For you maybe. Makes no difference to me.'

'Their web of influence makes the conspiracy hard to detect. Take Margot. The Security Commission meetings were held in secret. He knows, even now, the most sensitive areas of political and technological negotiations between Russia and the West.'

Smith listened without comment. It was for Blanc's ears.

McCall went on. 'The Commission dealt with security *formally*. Otherwise it covered many other things. Margot was in on all of it. He knows where to hurt the British government. Any government. And he's queer. He'd be useful to anyone. As it is he's not working for us alone.'

McCall breathed in deeply. 'Anyhow, it's the assassinations we're interested in. The rest of it can't concern us. There's not enough time.'

Blanc protested. 'Is this really all you're going to tell me? I must know some more.'

'It's all you need to know.'

'Well don't expect too much then.'

It began to rain and they turned back for the farmhouse. Blanc looked out at the fields. The soil had hardened, covering next year's growth—the weeds and grasses would be fighting each other. Last year's weeds still twined around the hedgerows by the drive. They were the same green as the other plants, only some weedkiller would sort them out. A man-made chemical was needed. Sheer violence might be too obvious.

On the day he left Blanc was given details of his journey to London. He was to leave the train at Reading, where a driver from the sub-section would meet him at a bus stop outside the station. This was apparently how they 'always did it'. He would be given further detailed instructions by Helmsman who would also make contact with him at the Club in good time.

It was still raining as they left the farmhouse. McCall drove, Blanc was in the passenger seat and Smith sat in the back.

They took the same road through the hills to Swindon as Blanc had taken on the motor bike. Instead of the queues outside the football stadium there was a solitary newspaper-seller huddled in a doorway with his legs crossed. A few yards away, under the canopy of the stadium stretched small rectangular boards in reds and blues, POOLS RESULTS. RACING. STATE BROTHELS IN AMSTERDAM.

'Poor sod,' McCall said, glancing at the newsvendor.

'I don't know,' said Smith, 'Amsterdam's looking up.'

'What did it say?' McCall strained round but had to look back quickly to clear the oncoming traffic.

He laughed.

'State brothels in Amsterdam,' said Smith.

McCall ignored the observation.

The train was in and Blanc wondered why they'd come to see him off. He felt like a schoolboy, or a voluntary patient being sent off for another stretch to understanding relations in the city.

McCall shut the carriage door for him.

'We'll meet again soon,' he said. Then he leaned through the carriage window close to Blanc's shoulder to see if there was anyone else in the corridor, '... don't abuse hospitality again. You're on your own.'

'What do you mean?' Blanc asked, amazed.

'It always hurts someone. Jean Mungo's body's been found. In a disused warehouse.'

Blanc stared at him wildly. 'What?'

'In a warehouse. It looks like suicide. It'll be an open verdict of some sort. Sorry about it, Blanc. Think you knew her didn't you?'

'You bloody well know I did.'

The train's hooter gave a blast. The guard was shouting. There was a lot of noise.

'Wasn't sure. But I am now. Murdoch. The Reverend Ian Murdoch followed you from The Lawn. She spent the whole night, all of it, at the farmhouse. It was a terrible risk. God knows man what she saw. Or even,' he said disgustedly, 'what you told her.'

Blanc looked at McCall with hatred.

'You've waited until now to tell me ...'

The train shook slightly. Smith was standing by the barrier.

'McCall,' Blanc spat out his name, 'shall I tell you something. You're a bastard.'

Blanc shivered. It sounded too little.

'Perhaps,' said McCall.

Carriage by carriage the train was moving out of the station.

7

Like most academics Blanc paid more attention to the newspapers than he was prepared to admit. In London he had soon forgotten the shortcomings of the heavily censored *Rudé Pravo* and he read the English papers and the weeklies avidly. He had found in Cambridge that what were usually described as central issues were the ones his fellow students had heard about too late. Or they had never really understood their origins. Not so Blanc. He had discovered what started Korea,—why the French had been in Vietnam,—who Lynskey was,—why the *Irgun Zvei Leumi* were reassembling in Israel,—and why the *Irgun* men had entered the King David Hotel in Jerusalem in 1946, and had blown it up and run for it.

He persevered in keeping up with current events and knew more about English politics, their history and curiosities than many of the English did themselves. All of which meant that he was particularly sensitive to his obligations to McCall. *Precisely because so much had been left unsaid.* Basically, if ever he had been pressed to say so, he would have admitted that he wasn't personally dedicated to Establishmentarian notions of English patriotism and nationalism. Now it was a little different: because he supposed that he was directly engaged in furthering them. But the vision of the body of Jean laid out on a mortuary table for identification appalled him. Why go that far?

A copy of the *Western Mail* lay on the seat opposite. Instinct made him pick it up. It was yesterday's. Most of it was devoted to the successes of the current Welsh Rugby Football team. On the second page a headline stood out in bold. 'Girl's Body Found. The body of Jean Rita Mungo, sixteen, of Queen's West Estate, Swindon, was found by police in a disused warehouse of British Rail in Swindon. Acting-Superintendent J. Grace said today that foul play had been ruled out. Death was from exposure.'

Blanc knew it was a lie.

Reading station was deserted apart from three uniformed porters sipping tea from paper cups by the exit. A clock in the main entrance hall had stopped and its hands had been moved round to twelve.

He followed his instructions and waited outside the station at the nearest bus-stop. Two couples came out of a pub opposite, the men wearing similar sheepskin coats.

'See you on Monday,' one of them said.

They went off in opposite directions.

A bus pulled up and some red-cheeked old ladies clambered off. One of them was clutching a large bunch of red gladioli.

Then they too walked away.

As he watched them go a voice behind him said quietly, 'Mr Blanc?'

He turned.

'I've a car waiting for you.'

McCall's sub-section never let its people take the train the whole way to Paddington. They drove to Reading first and the same applied to journeys in the opposite direction. Blanc was driven out of Reading with deliberation; the driver observed the speed limits with an official style of driving.

The driver left him in Jermyn Street and Blanc walked into St James's Square to the Royal Services Club, which was smaller than he had expected. Its stone façade was grey in contrast to the clean buildings in the rest of the square.

The walls of the entrance hall were covered with notice boards displaying regulations, resignations and deaths of members. The hall porter sat at a telephone switchboard beneath a large oil painting of Admiral Beattie. Some post-cards were slotted into the side of the telephone desk, most of them marked 'To Await Arrival'. There were none for Blanc. The porter looked up, and Blanc said, 'I think you've got a room for me. O. B. Blanc.' The porter wet his thumb and pulled over the pages of a long diary. 'Number thirty-five at the back sir.' He walked round from his desk.

'May I take your bag sir? I can't leave the desk for long.'
The bustling little man with his blue jacket stretched over his bent back led Blanc to the lift.
There was a stale smell of lunch in the place. It was dry and meaty. He took Blanc along a dimly lit corridor.
'Here you are, sir. Thirty-five. Here's your key. Dear, they can't have drawn the curtains.'
He minced to the window.
'Club servants aren't what they used to be sir.'
'I suppose not.'
Blanc wasn't sure whether he was meant to agree or not.
'Could I have some tea up here?' Blanc asked. 'Please.'
'It *is* Sunday, sir.'
'I know.'
'Just tea?'
'That'll do. Thanks for carrying the bag.' Blanc held out a clenched fist with two shillings in it.
But the porter just stared. 'I'm sorry?' he asked.
'I said thanks for carrying my bag.'
'Sir. The club rules. *Please*. No gratuities.'
He took a malicious pleasure in it.

The tea came. Eventually. The maid who brought it was a tall coloured girl. She had knocked only once on the door and had come in hurriedly. She wore an unfashionable black dress which fitted too tightly. But it served to accentuate a very striking figure and showed off her loping fluid walk.
'Over here, sir?'
She placed the tray on a brown mahogany writing desk. And then she walked to the door and shut it.
Blanc was taken aback. All he could think of to say was 'I didn't know this club had women too.'
'Only the maids,' she replied in a surprisingly cultured voice. 'You're Mr Blanc?'
'That's right.'
'I believe we're to work together.'
Blanc couldn't think what she meant. He suspected some kind of trap.
'On what?'
She looked at him quizzically.

'Surely ...' she began.

Blanc interrupted, 'What's your name?'

'Marcia Helmsman.'

'I see. I see,' Blanc said. 'Sorry. It was just that I didn't expect a coloured woman.'

'What do you mean?' she asked sharply.

'A woman. That's all.' Blanc was embarrassed.

She leaned against the door.

'Well, I hope you won't mind *too* much. I'm on duty on this floor every day. Ostensibly I tidy your room out. And bring you breakfast.'

'That's nice....'

'Good. You've come none too soon.'

Then she stood up straight and opened the door. 'I'll see you tomorrow.'

Blanc looked round the room. So he'd come none too soon.

He didn't much like what he saw. The cover to the bed was made of material more suited to curtains; brown and overcleaned, having a quality of utility about it like post-war radios and the children's clothes the British used to send to Prague as gifts in the '40s. It wouldn't wear out but it would always show the stains.

The room backed onto a space enclosed by office windows behind which he could see potted plants on the window sills. The brick walls were dirty and covered by fire escapes zig-zagging up and down. There was one rusting spiral staircase.

The room could never be fully lit by daylight, at least one electric light would always have to be on. It was really a stop-off for the ex-officer or the provincial businessman attending London meetings or reunions. Once its conventional occupant returned in the early hours he would find himself caught in a limbo. Caught between a feeling of relaxation from his domestic and working routines and the promises of a lone walk into the West End.

There, the prostitutes would still be trading. They held the promises of his walk and would make him give them up for a pound or two. A fierce release, a savage race of ten minutes to excitement. And then she would wipe the man dry like a baby. 'Thank you,' he would say, incongruously polite even in the most private of business deals. He would hurry down the stairs. In front of the bookshops the grills would be up and the Maltese or Cypriot doormen would be taking the strip-club displays inside for the night.

Or he might take the same walk but do no more than glance up the stairs beyond the notice PLEASE WALK UP. He would hurry back to St James's satisfied that he had kept other promises made to his wife.

Back in the brown room he could change his routine. He could visit the bathroom at night instead of in the morning, splashing in the outsize bathtub—the water stains on the enamel streaming down from the heavy taps to the plughole.

Or his vengeance on convention might be reaped even more privately—he could urinate in the basin in the corner of the room and wash it out elaborately. Why the hell should he walk down the passage to the lavatory?

The room depressed Blanc. He had expected it to have a masculine comfort. White sheets, rough stiff towels. Instead it smelt of tobacco and he pondered the talc which had thickened around the rim of the basin. Even the bolts holding the mirror to the wall had fine circles of bright green mould at their edges.

He had brought no files. Everything had to be remembered. There was no revision to be done.

He thought of the four men, each a member of this place.

He looked at his face in the mirror. And he considered that his energy was of a nervous kind. He had never felt the need for physical exertion. He had only so much energy, so he might as well preserve it.

He wondered about the interests of the members. Sex, usually. Sport, yes. He had never been interested in sport, except in the history of prize fighting. He knew that the strength of a blow struck with the naked fist is less than one with a four ounce glove. Although the effect of the first shows up more when the blood flows, the damage is external. But the effect of the glove is numbing, a deep bruise is more likely. It was the difference, if you like, between being cut with a blade and being hit with a club.

He disliked violence but it fascinated him. He would when the occasion demanded quote:

A hasty temper never show
Nor strike your little friend a blow.
Far better wait till you are cool
And then half kill the little fool.

He had remembered this when the KGB officer had fallen
backwards against the wall of the offices of the Czech
Communist Party, the blood streaming from a cut across
the top of his left ear. He hadn't stood a chance. He had
sunk surprisingly fast to the ground. The crowd had closed
in and Blanc had backed away into it, pushing and struggling
to get beyond. Once he made it he ran and ran and ran.

Thank God he hadn't been hired for murder.

McCall had told Blanc at the farmhouse that his flat in
Diadem Court had been left empty. According to McCall,
Blanc's few possessions had been taken by someone from
the sub-section to a furniture depository in Chiswick. 6
Diadem Court had been rented by the sub-section through
a firm of lawyers.

So if Busek tried to find out what had happened to the
previous tenant he would   be politely stalled. His search
would be made a little harder at every turn.

Blanc had brought Oppenheim's *The Great Impersonation*
with him from the farmhouse and when he had finished
reading it he thought he would have a look round Soho and
take in a visit to his old flat. He could find out for himself if
what McCall had said was true. Perhaps the new tenants
would give him some information about enquirers. There
was no other way to tell how close Busek was to him and
whether McCall was making real progress in 'fixing things'.

He left the club, avoiding the glance of the hall porter and
a group of members greeting each other heartily by the door.
He had to tap one of them on the shoulder to get through.

He crossed Piccadilly into Soho.

The familiar doormen were touting outside the striptease
clubs. The usual light shone from the first floor window of
'Jenny's room' in Wardour Street. Diadem Court was empty
and his flat was closed up. A padlock and bar had been
screwed to the doorhandle. A typed notice asked that all

60

enquiries be made to Messrs Payne, Patch and Heim at an address in Bedford Square.

He tried the door, shook it twice and gave up.

Outside he stood in the doorway. Soho, he reflected, was still the measure of London even if it was only a barometer of libertinage. There were signs that the clubs were now being eclipsed once and for all by the slot-machine palaces. But the restaurants continued, and the out-of-work waiters still queued outside the bars.

If Soho was a measure it was also a kind of sieve. Some people worked there just before giving up to drink, or the needle, or to a racket of one sort or another. These people fell through the sieve. They were eventually forgotten for they hadn't registered their work: they were professionals but without pensions, without state benefits.

Looking out from the doorway he wondered what the other residents of Diadem Court had seen from behind their muslin curtains.

The last person he had seen was Smith, whose 'friends' had watched him for months. He wondered who they were. There would be facets of his character and beliefs that they wouldn't know about. Should he tell them that he was now unsure of his Marxist convictions? That his beliefs lay somewhere to the right of the old Czech Communist Party line. That he remained a convinced Socialist nevertheless? No. He decided he would let the shadows of the sub-section find that out for themselves. The distinction between feeling and imagination was a fine one; mainly because the work of a shadow thrived on suspicion and suspicion thrived in turn on imagination.

And all that was their problem.

He gave himself the pleasure of looking out at Diadem Court once again before he left.

The two streetlights at the end of the court were out. He looked into the darkness and at the lampposts.

Then he saw the figure.

He was standing back in a doorway.

For a brief moment they both became aware of looking at each other. Blanc instinctively realised that the figure was there because he was. He tried to see the man's face. But he was well back and there wasn't enough light. If it was someone from the Embassy or the sub-section he just might have seen the face before.

He decided to walk towards the figure and see what happened.

Whether his plan had become obvious to the other man or not he could never tell. But, without looking up, the figure darted sideways from the doorway. He sprinted into Berwick Street.

Blanc gave chase. Their footsteps clattered through the courtyard but even in the short distance Blanc was outpaced. He could see the man's short three-quarter-length blue coat. He swore at the lighting. But it was no use and the figure vanished in the direction of Regent Street.

Blanc leant against a barrow in Berwick Street Market to get his breath back. He bent down, panting.

He went back slowly to Piccadilly and, to avoid the traffic made for the underground which would bring him up on the other side.

It was outside the entrance that he noticed the same blue coat again. The stairs leading down to the ticket hall were crowded. Blanc let the man go down ahead of him and kept him in sight.

When he reached the ticket hall packed with homegoers, some West Indians slipped between Blanc and the man in the blue coat.

The blue coat couldn't have been more than ten yards away.

Blanc pushed his way forward.

Everyone seemed to be going against him. He pushed with his elbows, his arms and his hips. People didn't like it.

'Hey. Excuse me....' he called.

But the man didn't hear and was disappearing again. It was no good. Blanc couldn't reach him. The man turned and made for an open space next to the entrance to the Men's Lavatories.

Blanc was directly in front of them when he felt a stabbing pain in his kidneys.

He stepped forward, gasped, half-turned. There was a hard collision against the back of his neck. Someone's fore-arm, he felt the hard bone. He tried to run. Another blow on the back of his head. His head was filled with noise, like an echo unexplained.

Then his knees gave way. He choked, and passed out.

He came to sitting on the floor of the lavatories. He had vomited on the floor and a uniformed ticket inspector was flicking water in his face from a basin. 'O.K. Take it easy. ...' he was saying.

Blanc looked up. He tried to focus. His head ached violently.

'Who was it?' he murmured.

'I don't know. I didn't see it. The first I knew was seeing you on the floor.'

'Where?'

'Outside.'

'No. Where did they go?'

'No one saw them.'

'You mean no one tried to stop them?' Blanc's head throbbed.

'People mind their own business.'

Blanc tried to get up.

The inspector looked down at him. 'Do you want me to get a doctor?'

'No. I'll be O.K.' He lifted himself up onto one arm but felt too faint to get up on his own. The inspector pulled him gently to his feet.

Blanc managed to reach for the basin and doused his face in water. It cleared his head.

'I'll manage,' he said. 'Thanks for your help.'

The lavatory floor was wet with disinfectant and Blanc half-slipped on the tiles as he pulled at the automatic towel machine to clean himself. The other men hurrying in and out adjusting their trousers looked at him with distaste. Either he was drunk or unpleasantly ill.

Very uneasily he went slowly back to St James's Square.

Marcia Helmsman brought him breakfast the next morning. She shut the door after her, and left the curtains drawn.

'How are you?' she asked.

'I don't want that,' Blanc replied, looking at his breakfast.
'What's wrong with it?'
'I've a terrible headache.'
She sat down at the side of his bed. 'What's wrong?'
'Not much. Someone beat me up in the Piccadilly tube station.'
'Where were you going?'
'Damn that,' Blanc said with accusation. 'I wasn't going anywhere. I was coming back here.'
'You look all right to me,' Marcia said, as if to apologise
'That's because you can't see the after effects. I can feel them though.' He ran his fingers across the back of his neck. 'And in the small of the back too.' He winced.
'So what happened?'
'Someone was following me. I followed him. Lost him. And then before I knew it I was smashed on the head and woke up in the Gents.'
'Didn't anyone help?'
'Of course not. They never bloody do. There was just an inspector who brought me round by throwing water at me.'
'All right then, lie back. I wouldn't worry. Maybe you were mistaken for someone else.'
'I doubt it.'
'I wouldn't worry.'
She smiled at him quietly.
Her lips were slightly black and purple and a rim of soft red appeared around her teeth as she smiled. Her skin was a dark copper colour, probably the result of an inter-marriage some generations back. This would have explained her long soft hair which gave the appearance of being a wig but wasn't. Her dress really was too tight especially across the breasts.
'You don't really look so bad,' she said.
'Maybe,' Blanc replied with deliberation. 'But I don't at all like being beaten up for no reason at all. It's very scary.'
'That's the point. Most likely someone was trying to scare you. Feeling you out perhaps. Just intimidate you. It wouldn't be the first time it's happened to someone in the sub-section.'
'That's nice to know.'
'I'll put in a report. They might have an idea about it. At

any rate they'll want to be told. Where does it hurt?'

She leaned over him. Her hair brushed against his face. Blanc could smell a light perfume. He shifted onto his side.

'It's better than it was.'

'Can you concentrate then? Just briefly.'

'O.K.'

She took out a small white envelope from the pocket in her dress.

'This is a hearing device.' She broke a wire seal at the top of the envelope and tipped out a small circular plastic object onto the bed. It looked like a button.

'You're to plant this on Donnelly. It's wavelength is preset. You make it effective by pressing this.'

She sat on the bed and showed him a small red mark on the device.

'It automatically releases a mechanism to make it adhesive. It won't stick to you. There's a time switch to let it take effect gradually after you press on the mark. That's all you have to do to prime it.'

Blanc picked it up. It was incredibly small. She watched him turn it over in his hand.

'Simple enough,' he said. 'What were you doing before this?'

'I was in Jamaica. My father's in the government.'

'Nice.' He looked at her.

'What else have you done for the sub-section?'

'Desk work. This is the first time outside the administration section.'

'Where's that?'

'In Victoria.'

She was undoubtedly attractive. Her lips shook a little as she spoke with a hint of maternalism. She seemed to care about his injuries even though she now realised they were relatively minor.

'And you?' she asked him.

'I've been invited in as it were. Ordered to volunteer. No option.'

'I heard about it.'

'I expect you know more about me than I do.'

'Perhaps.'

'It wouldn't surprise me. They seem to have got half London wandering about after me.'

'You'll have seen photos of Donnelly and the others.'

'Some of them. They're following me too?'

'I doubt it. Not yet.'

'Well, we'll find out when I go to Donnelly's place.'

'It's worrying you.'

'Of course it's worrying me. I'm bloody scared.'

'There's no need to be. After all, it's not burglary. You're giving him something, not taking anything, and you're getting paid for it.'

'Thanks a lot,' Blanc said sarcastically.

'Makes it better though.'

They laughed.

'Do you want to ask any questions before I go?'

'Yes. Just out of interest. I'd like to get a look at Donnelly before I plant this thing.'

'That's easy,' Marcia said, brushing her hair from her face. 'He'll be playing roulette in the Card Room tonight, probably on his own. He usually leaves about two a.m. and drives back to his house along the Great West Road. It takes him about forty minutes. So your best time to get inside will be between one and two o'clock.'

'What's the best way to approach the house?'

'It's three hundred yards from the Twickenham side of Richmond Bridge. It's set well back from the river in the trees. The best approach is to cross the bridge and follow any of the roads running parallel to the river. Donnelly's house stands on its own. It's called Edgerton House, but avoid arriving at the front. Come at it from the river side. You'll see a large green gate—but don't climb it because he's fitted an alarm that runs round the edges. It's highly sensitive. Go to the right of the gate, through some rhododendrons and over the wall.'

'Where exactly is the best place to fix the device?'

'You may have to look around once you're inside the house. But if you can, fix it under the top of the large desk in the lounge.'

'O.K. and how do I get there—by taxi?'

'No. Go via Waterloo by train. One leaves about midnight.

If anyone's following you you'll have a better chance of shaking them off. Use the old ploy of getting in and out of carriages to see if your shadow follows you. At Richmond walk to the bridge, you'll find your way from there all right.'

'What about seeing Donnelly beforehand? Tell me again.'

'Just go to the Card Room and hang around at the back.'

Marcia leant back slightly on the chair and pulled her skirt over her knees.

'When do I see you again then?' Blanc asked.

'Tomorrow morning. If you don't want an early call ask the porter to see you aren't disturbed. There'll be a relief porter on duty when you get back.'

She stood up once again straightening out the black dress. 'All right?'

'Yes,' Blanc said, looking her in the eyes.

Once she had gone he got out of bed, stretching himself to try to relieve the stiffness in his back. It wasn't too bad after all. Next time, though, they might do a better job.

By the time he had positioned himself in the telephone box in the hallway opposite the porter's desk he no longer noticed the pain of the night before.

Donnelly arrived alone. Just to look at him one would have guessed he'd been an Army officer. Not of course that he marched with his bottom out like a warrant officer; Donnelly strolled casually in, almost effeminately. His face was closely shaved and shining, his hair swept back and brilliantined. When he took off his hat his hair was left with one wave in it.

He handed a briefcase over the desk to the porter and said something which Blanc couldn't hear. Then he walked slowly to the stairs and out of Blanc's range of vision, a self satisfied, somewhat indolent but affectedly authoritative man.

When Blanc entered the Card Room no one looked up. There were many more men in the room than he'd expected; about a dozen of them sat round an oval table covered in green baize, their faces lit by a clear light in a large pyramid shade. The whole table was in a cocoon of light in which trailers of blue cigar smoke drifted slowly upwards. Trouble had been taken with this room at least; the chairs were upholstered in red leather and the carpet had a thick pile to it. Even the waiters wore stiff white jackets with a crest on the breast pocket.

'*Faites vos jeux, messieurs, faites vos jeux....*'

Donnelly sat in the centre of the table, his hands around a large cut glass of whisky.

'Doubling up again, Donnelly?' someone said.

Blanc stood back in the shadows and watched Donnelly's chips scooped away. The roulette wheel was spun once more, the little balls clattered around the figures like a rider on a wall of death. '*C'est le numéro ... neuf, c'est neuf, messieurs, impair et rouge, impair et rouge.*' And this time Donnelly won.

Blanc had a reasonable impression of what Donnelly looked like, so he left the room and went to the Club bar downstairs.

At eleven he returned briefly to the Card Room to take another look at Donnelly before leaving. As Blanc walked round the table in the shadow he noticed not only that another croupier had taken over, but that Donnelly wasn't there. There was a chance that he'd gone to the washroom. Blanc waited. But Donnelly didn't return. He couldn't wait any longer. He decided to take a chance on Donnelly not having reached his house before he managed to break into it.

He was doubly uneasy on his way to Waterloo and he hoped wildly that Donnelly wouldn't be waiting for him. Once or twice he looked round suddenly to see if anyone was following him, but they weren't and he felt rather foolish. Yet still the violent anonymous attack of last night played on his mind. Who the hell was it? Busek, Donnelly's people or even McCall's sub-section trying him out? There seemed to be no reason for the first and last suppositions.

He looked round again as he bought a ticket only to look straight into the face of an elderly woman with blue tinted hair.

He realised he knew so very little about this so-called sub-section.

Blanc was the only person in the carriage as it rocked and

swayed westwards, just before midnight. In Richmond he followed Marcia's instructions. He walked through the town still looking round to see if anyone was close behind. He turned over the bridge and looked down at the blue-black river beneath. The roads beyond were in almost complete darkness, the wind catching the large beech trees, blowing the leaves hard down into the road and swirling them along. A dog barked irritably at him through a gate and made him jump. Most of the houses were hidden by the trees but in some of them he could see a light in an upstairs room and a figure move fleetingly behind a curtain.

The dog barked on, then eventually stopped.

High up the clouds skidded across the sky letting through enough light for him to find the footpath which veered sharply left. He saw the gate in front of him. He could not remember whether Marcia had said it was green or blue, and what confused him further was another gate in the wall just visible from where he was standing. It must have been some thirty or forty yards to his right.

He decided to climb the wall, which was a mixture of grey and rust crumbling brick; where it had been patched up hastily the cement protruded and it would give him something of a foothold. It was a little over twelve feet high which meant that he had to take a short run, secure a brief foothold and then reach for the top. His first attempt failed and he grated the inside of his wrists on the rough brick. The second time he found his grip and managed to pull himself up onto the top of the wall and sit briefly astride it. He peered at the house, and saw that about fifty yards of lawn and shrubbery lay in front of it. He edged his stomach across the ridge of the wall, noticing that purely by chance he had chosen his point of entry well. Either side of him the top of the wall was made up of cement mixed with short lengths of barbed wire and bits of broken glass. Dangling from the top of the wall he let himself drop; six feet between the ground and someone's shoes is a long way to drop in the dark and Blanc landed heavily on his side in a bed of cut back nettles.

He made his way towards the house up one side of the lawn. He had completely forgotten that houses could be sinister, that they could frighten at first sight. Small houses usually do not scare, unless they are derelict and with traces of people who have left them recently.

But Donnelly's house was sinister simply because it was huge and in darkness, its windows tall and unusually narrow; they gave the house a suggestion of ecclesiastical purpose.

As he walked nearer along the edge of a curved flower bed he could see that the walls were faced with smooth stone. Predictably two large floor to ceiling windows were situated in the centre of the ground floor; a flight of low steps ran up to them from the garden.

He felt completely exposed.

If someone was to look out of any of the windows he would be seen with ease. Once up against the windows above the steps he felt that to open them would be senseless; if Donnelly had wired up one of the gates he was sure to have wired up the windows as well. He looked back down the garden and decided to try the windows; if the alarm went off he would run for it.

He pressed the button on the bugging device in his jacket pocket and turned the handle on the window.

It was locked but as he pulled the doors they came slightly apart, obviously one of the bolts had not been secured. He pulled again but they wouldn't move. He pulled again a third time and the door opened with a sharp clatter. He stepped through the windows, pushing the thickly lined curtains to one side.

He felt his way forward into the room and banged his knee against a chair. Standing still, waiting to get his eyes accustomed to the darkness, he could begin to make out the room: large glass bookcases along one wall, a television set on a trolley and just beyond the large oval desk. He walked slowly towards it, the device in one hand, the other out-stretched in front of him. Bending down by the desk he stopped again and listened.

There was a slight creak, it might have been the door to the garden swinging in the wind. He was quite still. He listened again and heard another noise, either a creak of a floor board or a handle turning in a door. It came again, it might be in the room. Perhaps there was someone in there with him. He was now sweating, his collar stuck to his neck and he wiped his forehead with the back of his wrist. He stretched out under the desk and pressed the device against it, where it held firmly in position. He was kneeling on the carpet, staying quite still; there were just fifteen or sixteen feet between him and the window. The creak was quite loud this time.

He decided to run.

He sprinted for the window, a chair fell backwards and he heard it hit the floor as he jumped the steps to the garden. The lights came on. He weaved his way down the lawn. Three shots rang out in quick succession, spitting into the lawn, just to his right. He weaved and bobbed furiously, then some six or seven shots tore into the path just behind him.

Then he was back in the shrubbery in front of the wall. He glanced back sharply. Lights had gone on in the drawing-room and he could see a man coming fast towards him, a rifle still in his hand.

He stood back from the wall for a moment and then took a run at it, found a footing between the bricks and heaved himself up. But he had grabbed at some barbed wire which cut into the palm of his hand. There was nothing to do except pull himself up, although the blood already full and warm was flowing freely back down inside his jacket sleeve. He whimpered, tore the front of his trousers and fell down onto the footpath the other side.

He was badly winded and his hand was going numb.

He ran down the footpath without looking back. He thought he heard a car start up beyond the wall but he kept on running.

He decided to make for the river. He suddenly realised that the man with the rifle had been Donnelly. Presumably he had reached his home at the same time as Blanc. Or maybe he had expected Blanc and somehow knew what was going on. Blanc put it down to coincidence.

On the other hand Donnelly *had* left the roulette table earlier than usual.

At least the device was in place. All he had to do was get to the station. And he was feeling very faint.

He clutched his wrist, trying to stop the flow of blood from his hand. But the blood still dripped onto his clothes as he half walked, half ran down to the platform.

The only other people on the 2.24 a.m. to Waterloo were four railwaymen with shadowed faces and canvas bags.

Blanc let himself into his room at half past three in the morning. He found that Marcia had left a bottle of whisky on the writing desk. In the space of half an hour he drank it all, occasionally dipping a face towel in his glass and dabbing it onto the open cut on his hand, feeling it would somehow disinfect it.

As he looked at the angry gash his main concern was that he might catch tetanus. When he finally managed to stop the bleeding he could see that the curve of the wound ran from the base of his forefinger almost to his wrist. It was a long red line and the white skin at its edges was turning up. The whisky calmed his nerves. He began to feel a thickness behind his eyes.

He was unsteady on his feet.

He felt very much alone. He remembered the don's wife and Jean and he also thought of Marcia.

His thoughts were incoherent and mixed up with vivid fantasy.

Jean and Marcia stood together in front of his eyes. He saw them naked. One of them was undressing, dark and light. Marcia seemed forbidden but she was so gentle.

Pulling the covers from the bed he turned out the light.

He watched the curtains. They hung still. He was working up an anger. He usually did when he was drunk.

He swore mutely at the club. It smelt of the English upper classes. Of toilet preparations. Of mothballs on tailor-made suits well preserved by nervous wives.

Sweating, he heaved himself from the bed and rummaged in his suitcase to find a handkerchief. He wound it round his hand.

There was still the uncertainty of action near at hand.

He wanted to use the lavatory. He turned the light on and found himself examining his face in the mirror. He noticed no change, except that he looked terribly pale. Not surprising. Twice in two days he had been near death: the attack in the tube station—he could recall the square patterns on the ceiling of the ticket hall. It had swayed, tilted and then tipped itself sideways.

He gripped the basin.

Only a few hours ago a dozen bullets at least had ripped up the grass around his feet thudding and whining off into the night. He could still feel the vibrations.

How could it be worse?

A bullet smashing into his ankles, a kick in the groin with a metal tipped shoe. More bullets. His ankles smashed at the bone whilst he lay screaming on his back, howling like a mad wolf in the Tatras—the blood running from his body.

His hand was throbbing up his arm.

He must have climbed back into bed without knowing it because he woke from a disturbed sleep suddenly. Dawn was breaking over London and he staggered to the basin and was violently sick.

When he next woke the empty whisky glass and bloodied handkerchief were where he'd left them and the curtains were still drawn. It was light outside.

Unknowingly he had tied a makeshift bandage around his hand. It was dry and heavy. Then he remembered tearing a handkerchief and bandaging his hand with difficulty the night before.

When Marcia eventually came to his room she told him it was three in the afternoon.

Blanc realised he had a powerful hangover.

'I feel as though I slept all last night in the park.'

'Show me it,' Marcia said, pointing at his hand.

She said something about a syringe, anti-tetanus and stitching. Blanc said it would need a doctor and she told him she'd been a nurse.

Despite the pain he fell asleep once more.

When he next awoke Marcia had brought him a meal and the bitter taste had left his mouth. He felt hungry.

She washed his hand, stitched it and gave Blanc an

injection in his rear. 'It'll get in the bloodstream quicker,' she said.

She might have been a nurse once but the jab hurt him. 'Careful. For God's sake.'

'Relax,' and she wiped his skin with some surgical spirit and cotton wool.

'Now you can tell me what happened at your bloody headquarters.'

'They're pleased.'

'*I should think so.*'

'Calm down,' she said. 'Eat this.' She pushed the tray towards him. 'There's some fruit juice. Scrambled eggs and salad.'

Blanc felt the sweet taste of the juice fill his mouth and gulped it down. He felt better. 'Is it all right for you to be here Marcia?'

'Fine.'

'Tell me what they said then.'

'The device is working all right. They're quite happy about it.'

'By they, do you mean McCall?'

'Yes. He started up again at the headquarters when you got here. Smith is there as well.'

'And you told them about the Piccadilly attack ...'

'Yes.'

'And what did they say?'

'They asked if you were all right. I said you were and that the shock had been worse than the blows.'

Blanc ate the eggs. 'And who was it?'

'They don't know. I don't think they're very worried. I told you. It's happened before. It's part of the trade.'

'How do you know?'

'Well, isn't it?'

Blanc did not know. He also discovered that Marcia didn't either. They weren't only freelance, but virgin freelance. Marcia said, 'McCall was very preoccupied. Far more so than I've noticed before. He was really quite sharp with me. I just couldn't see why he wasn't worried about you.'

Marcia looked coyly and surprisingly fondly at him.

'You can't expect him to be,' Blanc said. 'He's a cold sod.'

'But he *should* worry,' she said with intensity. 'From a personal and a practical point of view.'

'What do you mean *personal*?'

'You know what I mean.' She looked slightly embarrassed.

'It's all part of the game,' Blanc said tiredly.

Marcia picked up his case. 'You haven't unpacked this.' And she took out a spare shirt, socks and washing things. She arranged the contents of the bag in the chest of drawers near the basin.

'How well do you know McCall?' she asked.

'Hardly at all. I don't really want to either. Why?'

'I think he's got something else on his mind.'

'It's natural.'

'No. You wouldn't know what I meant....'

'I wouldn't pay any attention. Come and sit over here. Have some of this....' Blanc held out some toast.

'Tell me what you do here.'

'I make the beds in the rooms next door, bring the old boys breakfast. They don't like it.'

'The breakfast?'

'No. Being brought it by a coloured girl. I worry them.' She smiled.

'Do you really ...' Blanc laughed. 'How?'

'They don't like being seen in bed by a coloured girl.'

'So that's what you're employed by the sub-section for ...'

'No. I just report back to the sub-section whenever Donnelly and the others visit the club. And I'm here as a contact for you.'

'And that's all ...'

'Yes. It's been full time. Except in the summer.'

'What do you do then?'

'Sometimes I go on the river. The Thames. I take a launch from Windsor, usually on my own. It'd be good to go with you. Would you come?'

'Of course.'

'They always give me the same launch—the *Hanover Gold*. She's beautiful. The boatyard's a real mess—canvas strung up on ropes in the sheds, coils of rope, old fruit boxes. Just a mass of scattered junk. *Hanover Gold*'s terrific. Really. You'd love her.'

'Who do you go with?'

'No one. I go on my own. One of the boatmen asked to come too. He told me I was beautiful and matched the boat.' Marcia smiled. She fingered the bed cover and Blanc noticed how white the palms of her hands were.

'Who else thinks you're beautiful?'

'I don't know.' She looked thoughtful. 'One person—a girl.'

'A she?'

'Yes. About two or three weeks ago. In Chelsea. Two girls came up to me both in trousers and one of them in a sort of anorak with her hair brushed down. "Hey spadey," she shouted, rather bawled. "You're sweet, spadey." I ignored her. Then she laughed. I told her to shut up.'

Marcia shifted uncomfortably on the bed.

'You're not very curious.'

'Why, should I have been?'

'Yes. You should have found out what they wanted.'

'No thanks. I'm not like that.'

'You're the same about the sub-section. You should be more curious about it. Find out *exactly* what it is they're after.'

'I'm not paid to be curious. Not about the sub-section. I'm just a link between you and them. That's all.'

They sat silently. There was something innocent about her that Blanc found compelling. She was without danger and inspired a brashness in him that was uncharacteristic.

'You're not even curious about me?' he said petulantly. He hadn't meant it to sound like that, but it did.

'I do believe you're vain,' she said.

She was looking at him tenderly.

Then, very slowly, almost with resignation, she lay down next to him. She ran her fingers along his mouth. After a while she stretched back on the pillow.

Blanc wanted to hold her. 'Marcia,' he said quietly.

'Not now,' she said. 'Later. Why don't you stay in England?'

'It's not in my hands.'

'How do you feel about it now?'

'After that? Well, I don't think I have to say.'

Blanc looked at her tenderly.

'What about you?'

'It's no place for a coloured girl. I wish it was, but there are some strong undercurrents. It's all right for you.'

'I'm not sure. Look, McCall's traded on the fact that we're both aliens. I'm an émigré because I'm Czech—I've left somewhere, so they feel sorry. Or they say they do. Politely.'

'What about me then?'

'It's different. You're an immigrant. Because you've come here they feel threatened. There's a subtle difference.'

'I'm not sure I see it.'

Blanc paused, and laughed.

'But the English don't want to understand it. They find it best to read between the lines. Never the lines themselves. Someone in Cambridge told me that.'

'Doesn't mean to say it's true.'

'Maybe not. But it's half true. See what I mean?'

Blanc put his arm around behind her head and they lay silent again.

Marcia had set off recognisable reactions in him; he knew the restlessness in his legs. 'Can you stay Marcia?'

'No.'

'Why not?'

'Because.'

'Because what?'

'Just because.'

He felt he should thank her for bandaging his hand. But it would sound sentimental. It had been different with the don's wife, there had been a brief progression towards getting her into bed with him. With Jean Mungo it had been different again. He had felt something approaching sympathy for both of them. But Marcia was powerful; she would play it her own way, when she was ready and not before. Jean Mungo had ended up poisoned or strangled or both in a railway warehouse, the victim of an official murder. Marcia would manage to escape.

He could feel her hips against him through the bed clothes and her breasts pulled down tightly by her dress. Blanc pressed his mouth against her ear:

> 'Abstinence sows sand all over
> The ruddy limbs and flaming hair,
> But Desire Gratified
> Plants fruits of life and beauty there.'

'Did you write it?' she asked.

'No. I did not,' Blanc laughed. 'I'm not sure who did. Blake, I think.'

'One day perhaps.' Marcia said. 'Perhaps.'

She shifted herself off the bed.

'Stay here and rest your hand,' she added.

'Making love helps to heal,' Blanc said.

'That's not proven. Rest is better. Anyway, tomorrow you've got to meet McCall at the Strand Palace. At midday. He's giving you your next instructions.'

Then, for a short while, she lay on top of him again with her arms around his neck and kissed him.

They already shared something even if it was a joint escape from fear.

8

The foyer of the Strand Palace Hotel had recently been redecorated, updated and lit from the side, as opposed to from above, as it had been since the war. It smelt sharply of carpets, synthetic coverings and the small cigars of provincial businessmen.

People bustled in the foyer.

A neat man in white overalls struggled with a light fitting behind the news-stand at which Blanc turned over the pages of *Time*.

Five minutes before McCall was due.

Blanc turned to an overloaded circular book rack. He tilted his head to read the spines of the paperbacks. The man in white overalls finished his adjustment, closed his toolbox and walked off as neatly as he was dressed. Blanc kept his eyes half on the books and half on the revolving doors.

A figure paid off a taxi in the Strand. Richard McCall pushed his way into the foyer.

'How's the hand?'

'It'll be all right,' Blanc assured him.

'Let's have a look.'

McCall looked at the bandage.

'Is it painful?'

'Not as much as I thought it would be.'

'Not enough to put you off lunch?'

'No.'

'O.K. I'll get a taxi.'

The doorman outside whistled and waved. A cab drew up. McCall and Blanc got in and the taxi pulled out into the traffic.

'So ... so far so good,' said McCall.

'It wasn't quite what I'd expected.'

McCall nodded.

'We'll just hope that Donnelly thought he'd surprised a burglar. You did pretty well to get it fixed as quickly as you did.'

'Thanks for the compliment,' Blanc said.

The taxi pulled up at the lights in front of Waterloo Bridge. Blanc gazed out at the lunch hour crowds.

'How are you getting on with Helmsman?' asked McCall.

'Fine. It works well.'

He wasn't going to tell McCall anything else. He was learning the game. Need to know. Just tell McCall all he needed to know. No more. No less.

The traffic streamed over Waterloo Bridge. St Paul's was crisp and bright. The most sensual dome in Europe, Blanc thought.

On the other side they turned left.

McCall had booked a table for them in a small riverside restaurant overlooking the river. It was just beyond the *Daily Mail* warehouse.

Why, Blanc wondered, didn't the English love the Thames a little more? This was the London *he* loved and not just because it reminded him a little of Prague. The barges were being towed passively downriver to the Port of London. They lay flat and low in the water, a regular curved wave around their bows, quiet and serene. The barges were honest boats, solid, grand vehicles; in contrast to the chunky tugs. Blanc was captivated.

McCall gripped his elbow.

'So far so good,' he said again. And they went into the restaurant on the first floor.

A plump motherly waitress brought them soup.

The restaurant was too hot. Blanc looked out over the river. He couldn't see the barges, just the dark timber beams in the ceiling and the glare from the windows. McCall had his back to the light, and he smiled, but with his lips shut. It was patronising yet authoritative, the master-servant smile giving away just a little, a very little charm. He never moved his eyes and only slightly shaped the words on his lips. Like a ventriloquist.

'Bloody awful soup,' he said.

It seemed perfectly all right to Blanc.

'So you're progressing,' McCall said.

'Well enough.'

'You don't mind working on your own.'

'I never have before, I mean I never *minded* before.'

'So you do now?'

'No, not the part on my own. That's to say, I don't much care for what you're making me do. But ...'

'But what?'

'Well. I've no choice. We've been through it before.'

'We have. But I wouldn't look at it like that. You're doing the country a service.'

'Whose country?'

'This one.'

'Which isn't mine. Is it? I'm doing it for *myself*. Not for your country, not for mine, not for anyone's.'

'It's a pity you look at it like that.'

'That's your worry. Not mine,' Blanc said.

There was something in McCall which allowed him to persuade himself that such things *were* done for one's country. The service to patriotism. It wasn't nationalism, but patriotism. And it was indefinable. It was always thought a good idea in the Foreign Office to find out if candidates really wanted to do the job. If they didn't they'd be no good. It didn't matter how ambitious the candidate was, how much the Foreign Office meant in the eyes of fond relations. It just mattered that the man *wanted* to do it. Why?

Because that meant patriotism. It was as simple as that. Somewhere in every candidate the Empire urge crouched; it irritated, it burned, it pushed. And the Foreign Office was its salve.

But with a freelance it was entirely different. Bribery held its appeal for the petty criminal, the grafter, even sometimes the smoothie. But it didn't work with the intelligent, the sensitive or the intuitive man with an ability or potential for diplomacy. Yes, it was still diplomacy. In a new dimension. This was the dimension of weakness. If weak yourself you play on the weakness of the opponent and you can even get a candidate in on his weakness. The most suitable one is the faulted past. The hunted, the fear of the hunter. Basically the best candidates hate the hunt. But their desperation makes them follow it. So too Blanc.

Nevertheless McCall wanted more, he wanted Blanc to feel he really did want to do his job. It was the desire of the old lover. Above all *he* wanted to be wanted. Then he could summon up those imagined reserves of potency. And they never came.

So nothing would convince Blanc he wanted to do it. Why in hell's name should *service* interest anyone? Least of all the condemned man faced with the firing squad in the bowels of official Moscow.

McCall might seduce the young men from the universities. But never, never a Czech with the shattered confidence of a history decimated by invasions. A Czech who had charmed the rapist from the door only to find he ought to have owned a gun. Even though he didn't want to use one.

Fear was what ruled now. A terrible clarity of the inevitable.

Blanc may have been resigned to it but he wasn't going to tell anyone, let alone McCall.

They waited for the roast lamb in thick gravy, with a royal name.

'It's working rather well,' McCall said, 'the device you got into Donnelly's. I must say I am impressed.'

'Thanks. For that at least,' said Blanc.

'I think I should tell you to move around a bit more carefully. If that would appeal.'

'I've never said any of it appeals to me one bit, not one bit.'

McCall ignored it.

'You'll have to move circumspectly.'

'Why?'

'It's an occupational hazard. We might have foreseen it. In fact I suspected it myself.'

'What?'

'A double agent. There's just a chance they've dropped one on us. It's not hard to do if it's done slowly.'

'Who is it?'

'We don't know yet. But someone knows more about your activities than is healthy. But, then again, they might not be onto you specifically but onto someone in the sub-section.'

'How do you know?'

'Only in so far as you're concerned because it affects your movements.'

'So you've said.'

'What I mean is that they knew you'd go back to your flat.'

'I went on impulse.'

'I know but you went from the Club and you went back to the Club. They were waiting.'

'It could have been Busek.'

'It could. But I doubt it. He'll wait to strike at the most unlikely moment. Just you see.'

'But you said you'd fixed him...?'

'I didn't say I'd *fixed* anyone. Not exactly. We just used the political situation. Smith told you. The treaty. Sensitivity of negotiations. Busek's careful, so are his masters. The point is that someone's trying to intimidate you. And my conclusion, the more worrying aspect, is that they know something of what you're doing.'

'So it's more likely to be Donnelly?'

'Precisely. But they won't beat you up again. Sooner or later they'll approach you to find out what you know.'

'How?'

'You won't expect their approach,' McCall said. 'That's all you can be sure of.'

Blanc stared at him.

'You're not very comforting.'

The waitress polished the glasses at the next table. McCall glanced at her.

'It's not surprising there's a double agent,' said Blanc. 'He's probably quite humane compared with killers of young girls.'

McCall glared at Blanc, his lips quivering. He had scored an accidental hit right on target. McCall was hurt.

'Don't get bitter. It won't help.'

'So you admit it.'

'Think about yourself Blanc. Don't scratch.'

'Scratch.' Blanc raised his voice, 'Scratch. Christ. How dare you?'

'Don't raise your voice....'

'I hardly need to tell you I'm bitter—and with good reason.'

'Quite. We're offering you hospitality.'

'On your terms though. Strictly on your terms.'

'I wouldn't like to think there'd be a repetition of Jean Mungo.'

'That's up to you. It was incredible. And totally unnecessary.'

McCall was picking at his food.

The restaurant was filling up with men from the bar, who carried beer mugs and slopped them down on their tables, rubbing their hands with anticipation.

'There's a chance,' McCall said, 'that the double agent may try to reach you before the other three devices are in place.'

'So what do I do about it?' Blanc asked, frowning.

'We'll leave that for the present. I may reach him first. Wait and see. After all, you've been beaten up in the tube and shot at by Donnelly. The third time they may get you properly, unless we find him.'

Blanc adjusted the knife and fork in front of him. 'If they know me, what's the point of going on?'

'They don't know everything.'

'You haven't mentioned a double agent before.'

'No. There was no need to; but the risk increases when we employ freelance people.'

'Come on McCall. You didn't do so very well with your permanent staff.'

'If you mean Philby, then, as I told you, remember we've changed things.'

'I'm not sure they're better.'

'That's our affair.'

'Yes, but your excuses are lame. It's a good job you don't have to face your so-called free Press.'

'Philby did.'

'And he got away with it. I doubt you would.'

Perhaps Blanc had underestimated the target after all. McCall let him spend his ammunition. He sidestepped, swerved, parried gently and wriggled away from Blanc's unsophisticated attack.

The autumn sun glittered on the river, gulls were swooping down to the wakes of the barges. On the far bank the traffic lined up in a jam as far as Blackfriars. McCall followed

Blanc's gaze: 'We're keeping Marcia Helmsman at the Club. She can look after herself. You've just got Margot, Ames and Waterman to fix. In order please, Margot next.'

'Why?'

'That's the instruction. He's a bit odd, let's say he has odd habits.'

'Such as?'

'He might like you and he's not particularly lovely; rather bald except for a streak he brushes sideways against his parting. You'll be meeting him at Clapham Junction station.'

McCall handed him a Memorandum with directions to an address just off Whitehall next to the Ministry of Defence. 'The time for your interview there is written down. They'll want you to make contact within the next few days. A short briefing.'

'Who's the by-product this time, McCall?'

'By-product...?'

'I know you're killing off little girls, McCall, so who else gets it this time?'

'No one's killing off little girls. There's no evidence she was murdered. The police said something about exposure. We don't want you caught up with anyone else till you're through.'

Blanc had trapped him. McCall had after all killed Jean Mungo. In service. In the service of patriotism.

The men at the other tables began to shout.

The lunch had become uncomfortable. The food was dull, the whole place noisy and hot.

It wasn't the quiet instructive lesson McCall had hoped for. As for Blanc, he had asserted himself.

'What will happen to them once you've got the evidence?' Blanc asked.

'Well,' McCall said, 'what do you think?'

Blanc shrugged.

'I'll tell you, they'll probably be imprisoned for life, deported, which is the same as being part of a spy exchange deal, or I suppose they'll be disposed of.'

'Disposed of?'

'Yes.'

'This isn't the jig-saw you used to talk about.'

'Quite. It's not your business.'

'On the contrary.'

McCall pushed his chair from the table and crossed his legs.

'You're an idealist. An overwrought idealist. You could do with a bit more solid realism in your makeup. Think about yourself a little more. I do. I'm tired of living in hotels and I miss the Downs, in fact I miss a great many things. But there's a job to do. What happens afterwards, I don't know. It all runs deep, very deep.'

McCall ordered brandy. He became expansive, but it was a forced generosity and it succeeded in making him even more distant. Even this served as a disguise.

Blanc couldn't understand the tension. Perhaps McCall wanted to confide. Blanc couldn't tell. Anyway it would be embarrassing and wouldn't help either of them.

'Fill them up again,' McCall said.

More brandy.

He swirled it round with his hand cupped around his glass.

'We must meet when it's all over.' McCall turned his chair round and looked out over the river '... when it's all over.'

It was the only time Blanc had heard McCall speak with passion. Blanc couldn't miss the opportunity to reverse roles. He poured water on McCall's remark.

'Why not? In Moscow.'

McCall didn't appreciate the Czech black humour. He even affected not to have heard it. But Blanc enjoyed his own joke.

Yet he was sure that McCall's face had twitched. He *had* minded. Blanc could tell by the silence. It wasn't because of it that he kept quiet. His mind turned to Marcia, and to his payment. McCall couldn't be pressed. So Blanc kept quiet too, reluctant to draw any nearer Richard McCall's thoughts even if it meant that his curiosity would remain unsatisfied.

They pushed their chairs from the table. McCall got up slowly, and Blanc noticed that he was distinctly strained. He held onto the back of his chair a little too long and he quite noticeably screwed up his eyes. The leisurely confidence seemed to be shrinking. It occurred to Blanc, momentarily, that McCall might be grasping for self possession like a man troubled by acute mental exhaustion.

There was nothing more to say.

They would keep fear to themselves.

The double agent. Busek. Donnelly and the others, all, except Margot.

After all at least they knew Margot was just a queer.

9

Blanc felt a deep sense of resentment that the British government should have organised a highly efficient cell to study the London meeting places of homosexuals.

One man had been appointed to direct the operation. His two young assistants visited bars, theatre clubs, art cinemas and railway stations. They used cameras and tape recorders and even kept a map charted out with coloured pins. This was produced at executive meetings and enabled 'trends' and 'patterns' to be explained at a glance.

Blanc expected the man in charge to be some kind of disciplinarian. Instead he was confronted by a soft man with wiry red hair and blue eyes.

'One has to do unpleasant things. But actually they're never quite as nasty as you'd think.'

Here was a man with whom it was hard to reconcile McCall's bland theories of multi-level security. The same applied to the trio of Peeping Toms hanging around public lavatories poking cameras under partitions and securing tape recorders in ventilation grills.

'Much easier if we get to them before the others. Much easier for everyone....'

Blanc was brought a cup of sweet coffee. On the wall of the office was a large gold-framed print of Fonthill Abbey from Rutter's *Delineations of Fonthill*. Everything here had its connotations.

The man with the red hair had a freckled face. It was ageless like that of a well-preserved repertory actor.

'We very rarely approach them directly,' he said. 'Only when we're quite *sure*, if you follow me.'

'I don't.'

'We could become the seed-bed for the most vicious forms

of blackmail. Not of the department, but the victims. We approach them quietly, gently, with a certain suavity. We welcome them and give them a feeling of security. We record indiscretions and liaisons. Individuals are studied.'

Blanc saw it all: the noting of dates and places and the filing of the spectrum of bizarre physical contact and the photographs and sighings of homosexual love play.

'Surely it's illegal?'

'The ends justify the means.'

The man was without scruples. He had surrounded himself in cliché.

'I gather McCall wants this device placed on Clifford Margot. We can't do it. I've made it clear to McCall. Only in the most exceptional circumstances can we make a direct approach.'

'Placing a device doesn't involve that.'

'Of course. But we have to set it up and we haven't got the time. Nor the men.'

'Which is why I'm here.'

'I believe so.'

'So how do I do it?'

'You've two alternatives. First, the man's pressed. Personal and immediate difficulties. All sorts of things could happen. So you'll have to place it on him. It may not be so pleasant if you're not used to this sort of work.'

'I'm not.'

'Secondly, you may be lucky and find you can get what you want from Margot without the help of the device.'

'By doing what?'

'Using your head. Lead him on. A man his age wants company. And with what he's faced with he wants to talk. So let him.'

'What makes you think he'll say anything useful?'

'Intuition I suppose. He will, if I know the man.'

'Why don't you do it then?'

'I've told you. We dislike direct approaches. And I only know him from the files. I don't *know* him.'

'You are to go to Clapham Junction. The station. We've records on several of the regulars there. Margot's one of them. And he's regular. Within two or three hours. So get there about eleven. Margot's venue is Platform 2. Trains stopping, to Wimbledon, Chessington, Epsom, Kingston; and others passing through to Bournemouth and Salisbury. Margot's usual, a well established pick-up, is the 1.42 a.m. which stops at Hampton Wick. He might be earlier. You'll be fairly sure to get him on your first visit.'

'How can I be sure it's him?'

'You've seen the photographs. Surely?'

'Some time back.'

'Take a look at these.'

Blanc was handed three photographs in sharp focus.

'That's Margot,' the man pointed at the photograph with his thumb. 'And that's the solicitor's clerk. Margot's in trouble with him. There's a lot of talk in the chambers.'

'What's that?'

'His offices. Amongst his colleagues....'

'I suppose you're expecting me to deal with the clerk too.'

'No. He's away on holiday.'

'So what do I do?'

The photographs were replaced in a file.

'Mr Blanc.' The man pushed himself back on his chair and, as far as Blanc remembered afterwards, told him to be a man of the world. And then, in one sentence, told him that he was working for a high ideal, the peace of many and the hope of a free world.

Blanc arrived at the entrance to Clapham Junction an hour before midnight. At four minutes to eleven.

He bought a return ticket for Hampton Wick, and walked into the tunnel from which broad wooden stairs led up to sixteen platforms.

Margot might be there already.

Blanc didn't go to Platform 2 immediately. Instead he crossed the old covered walkway above the station.

It shook as a train passed beneath.

His footsteps echoed.

It was dimly lit and looked as if it hadn't been painted since the war. It was very damp. A row of windows at eye level enabled him to look out over the huge spread of railway lines beneath. They criss-crossed off into the distance towards London.

There were still a few lights on in the new blocks of flats beyond the station around Battersea and he could see the shadows of the warehouses and gasholders.

On the walkway he could hear someone else's steps besides his own. He was startled by two boys of about nineteen in pale blue trousers, very flared around the ankles, who walked past him holding hands. One of them wore a shirt with ruffles at the front and looked like a tall girl model.

He looked at Blanc knowingly.

Blanc watched them stop in front of the grill doors to a disused lift and then they both looked at him. Leave us alone their eyes said.

And Blanc walked hurriedly to the steps of Platform 2.

He could see that the glass partitioned shelters in the centre of the narrow platform were mostly empty. The lights were dim and wavered in the wind. It was even difficult to read a pink and black advertisement for a variety show at the Victoria Palace.

No sign of Margot.

From one of the shelters Blanc watched the trains slowing down. The diesel smoke puffed as the engines revved and they passed on south, their rear lights diminishing and disappearing. They left a faint smell of burned oil on the rails worn bright.

The station seemed unused.

Another train pulled in, doors slammed. Another diesel stirred its engines farther off.

Then the tannoy crackled into life. 'Delays of forty minutes will be experienced ... delays of forty minutes ... we apologise for inconvenience....' the announcement was repeated again echoing across the platforms. And it clicked off abruptly.

A man in a blue overcoat came down the stairs onto the platform. He stopped and peered along at the shelters. He approached a machine which sold sweets in bright cardboard cartons. Another man, much younger, in a denim suit joined him and together they shook the stand.

They spoke briefly. Blanc tried to hear what they said but they were out of earshot.

They sat down together on a bench, lit cigarettes and the

younger man started to laugh. Then they talked in whispers. Blanc ignored them. He directed his thoughts to how Margot would pick him up. He hoped he would because he himself wouldn't know how to make the first pass.

Would he be offered a cigarette?

A drink?

Or would it be the other way around?

What initiative would either of them take?

With fifteen minutes till 1.42 a.m. Blanc shivered. The red-haired man *must* be right.

Margot had to come.

And he did.

Blanc had an uneasy feeling of being stared at. It was a feeling he was used to. People had looked at him furtively in libraries and looked away even though he had not seen the watching eyes. He glanced down the platform again and saw the two men a few partitions away looking at each other. He also noticed a woman standing at the edge of the platform who bent down to open a small plastic carrier bag.

Someone was staring at him: not from Platform 2 but under a light on the platform opposite. Blanc thought he had caught his eyes and very pointedly he held his stare. He was able to make out Margot's bald head and the face which was darker than he had imagined. Margot walked quickly up the stairs to the walkway. Blanc saw him stop at one of the windows, look down and then walk on. He came on to Platform 2: Blanc stayed where he was. In different ways they had both been extraordinarily lucky.

'I've seen you somewhere before,' Margot said confidently.

'Yes,' Blanc said, 'yes, perhaps you have.'

'What's your name?'

'Dennis.'

'Dennis. Dennis. Yes. I'm sure we've met. What's the other name?'

'Dennis, that'll do.'

'Maybe we could take a ride. I'm on my way to Hampton Wick, there's a train due here shortly. I imagine you're waiting for a train too.'

'Yes. I am.'

'Let's go together,' Margot folded his arms across his chest tightly. 'Do you live alone?'

'Yes I do,' Blanc felt it was easier than he had imagined. Question and answer.

'I know how it feels. I've a small pied-à-terre in Hampstead, just off the Heath. Where do you live?'

'Around; in the West End,' Blanc said vaguely.

'Ah, nice. Hampstead's all right, easy to get to the practice.'

'Practice?'

'I'm a solicitor, very dull.' Margot was slightly nervous. 'Train's late,' he said.

Blanc would let him talk.

'They're changing everything here, they've even got round to scraping the paint off the glass roof to the walkway. It's been there since the blackout. Stations are changing. I'm fond of the railways, always have been. Nothing quite like the shunting stock, and the banks of signals; and if you look hard over there you can see the Ocean Liner Express being cleaned out.'

He was like a child. It had never occurred to Blanc that railway enthusiasts might be lonely and sometimes homosexual.

The train arrived. A coloured couple got out and slammed the carriage doors after them. Margot stood up directly the train came into the station and sought out a compartment which was empty. He also looked into the compartments at either side to see that they were empty too. He closed the carriage door and the train pulled out. Blanc looked through the windows of their compartment as they passed a signal box and noticed a kettle making a round patch of steam on the windows.

He wondered when exactly he should slip the device into Margot's pocket. It seemed absurd. The first time Margot turned his pockets out he would find it. All he could do was to get him to talk but he had no idea how to begin.

Four minutes out of Clapham with the train beating its way through the west London suburbs, Margot began to look Blanc in the face. Blanc noticed the slightly watery eyes, a little red around the rims, and stubble appearing on the chin.

'You're good looking, Dennis, you've an attractive smile, but you don't smile with your eyes.'

Blanc said nothing.

'I'm glad I met you Dennis. I felt instinctively it was right. I knew it. I saw you from over the platform. It wasn't that I'd known you before. Of course I hadn't. I just felt I had.'

Margot's breath smelt of stale French cigarettes. It was acutely unpleasant.

The train jogged on uncomfortably, passing close by the banks of a cutting, under a bridge, swerving over points; the clatter amplified in a tunnel, and out again, passing the ends of short suburban streets. Margot edged his shoulder close to Blanc's and pressed it hard against him. Blanc felt a tightness spreading in his stomach.

'Dennis,' there was a suggestion of pleading in his voice, of self pitying without the eagerness of a younger lover.

Blanc stood up.

Margot's mouth opened slightly, his eyes wide and questioning.

'Well...?'

'Not now,' Blanc said, 'not now please.'

'What's wrong?' Margot looked up at him.

'It's no good, I can't go any further.'

'I wasn't asking you to. I just want you to sit here.'

Blanc swallowed hard. He felt at a loss for words.

'Look, it's no bloody good. For a start I don't even know your name.' He realised this was a fatuous excuse. No one expected real names to be exchanged in these circumstances.

'It's Clifford Margot. Clifford please, not Cliff.'

'I've no objections to you personally, just not tonight.' Blanc felt near to abandoning the whole thing. And yet there was a wavering in Margot's voice. Perhaps it could be explained by Blanc's rejection.

The windows of the carriage streamed with condensation, Blanc was aware for the first time that it was too hot.

'Come on, Dennis,' Margot said. 'Come and sit down again.'

Blanc did not reply but stood looking out of the window through a blotch he had made on the wet glass with his sleeve.

They remained silent. The train pulled up at Putney where the station was quiet; a porter in a grey uniform with a red tie swept back over his shoulder walked past the window. The train moved out. Blanc turned and looked at Margot.

Margot's face was wet with tears. They ran down his cheeks. His lips were pinched tight and his neck, too, tightened up as he sobbed. Blanc was amazed, he had almost given in a few minutes before. He was frightened because he had had no idea how to respond to Margot's initiative, now the game had taken an unexpected turn. He had no idea how long it would take to get to Hampton Wick; maybe another twenty minutes. He decided to leave the train there anyway and return to London by taxi. Meanwhile Margot was in a railway carriage with him well past midnight and he would have to sit it out.

He sat down opposite. 'All right Clifford, tell me about it,' he said as if talking to a child. Margot sat up straight and pressed his head hard against the backrest.

'Christ. Oh Christ. It's just the strain of it, the strain.'

'Is that all?'

'No, not all by any means. It's just that I'm involved. You wouldn't understand if I told you.'

'I might.'

'I don't think so.'

'Well try to tell me then.'

Margot would have to be led on. The business of telling would have to be made attractive. Margot certainly seemed to be on the point of breaking. He was desperate to confide. It would be easier to do so to an anonymous pickup in the same way that prostitutes are easy to confess to.

'I'd get it off your mind,' Blanc said gently.

'I'm being got at.'

'That's not unusual.' Margot was breaking already. Blanc knew that understanding, a certain maternal sympathy would draw him on. 'It's blackmail, isn't it?'

'Yes, it is.'

'How many people are involved?'

'Several, more or less.'

'Tell me if it makes it easier.'

'A clerk, a solicitor's clerk in my office. I can't get out of it. We've been photographed together.'

'Where?'

'At my flat. I was bending over him.'

'Is that all?'

'That's all.'

'Well, you've nothing to worry about. It's perfectly legal. Presumably the boy's over twenty-one.'

'Yes, he's old enough. It's just, just that it looks so terrible.'

'That's your opinion. But is that *really* all?'

'No.'

Margot looked at him with the same beseeching look. 'No, it's not all. Not by any means. You wouldn't understand.'

'I might.'

'It's a political thing. A killing.'

'Come on, you're dramatising it.'

'No I'm not. A killing. And I know who.'

Maybe Margot knew that to almost anyone else it would sound mad, as if he had a persecution complex. In one sense he did. But it was what Blanc wanted to hear.

'I don't believe you.'

'It's all arranged and time's running out. I don't know what to do and I can't take it any longer.'

'Who's the victim?'

'I can't tell you.'

'Well, what sort of organisation is it you're involved in?'

'I can't tell you that either. I mean, I've been followed by people, there were those photos, so it goes on....'

Margot sighed loudly. His cheeks were still wet. Blanc did all he could to smile at him.

'You can tell me some more if you want to. Just something?'

'No, I can't I'm afraid. Really. I can't. I'm a professional man. That's all I've got left now. My professional reputation and the goodwill of a few old clients. But if they find out ... It'll all be lost.'

'But there must be more than yourself involved in the killing, you can't do it on your own.'

'That's true. Believe me. There are several people involved in it all. But anyway ...' he paused. 'Forget it. You don't want to get muddled up in this.'

96

'No. I don't. There's no reason why I should. It's just quite interesting.'

At this point Blanc knew that silence was his best tactic. Margot still wanted to let something out, but it didn't come. Then, as Blanc was on the verge of giving up and returning to polite conversation, Margot continued. It was as if he were talking to himself.

'It's because I was a superior sort of clerk to a sub-committee of the Standing Security Commission in 1963. I've kept in touch with some of the others who were on it. We meet from time to time. They're a nice lot. Then one day I was approached by a man in a London Club. Drinks led to drinks. He said I could be useful. Useful, that's what he said. That was four years ago. And this is where we are now. My life a wreck, a pointless mess. The killings, assassinations, murders—whatever you want to call them: these'll be the end of it.'

'Killings?'

'Yes, killings, assassinations.'

'You mean there'll be more than one? It sounds melodramatic to me.'

'Yes. Perhaps it does. Nevertheless ...'

Blanc stopped pressing him. And then looking at him hard tried once again:

'But who?'

Margot glanced petulantly out of the carriage window, 'I can't tell you. Honestly I can't. Please, don't press me any more. There's nothing that can be done about it.'

'All right I understand, but finally just tell me how it'll take place. You can mention that and you can trust me. After all, Clifford, it was me who smiled at you first. Wasn't it?'

Margot was pleased. It worked.

'The assassins' unit is to be armed in the most unlikely place at night three weeks from now. They drive the thirty or forty-five minutes to London, split up and then kill. Then there's a regrouping, a car to the airport and that's it. A private aeroplane's scheduled, quite legitimately, to take off for Dublin, then there's a switch of planes and they'll end up in Canada. Or they may go to Montreal direct. It'll all be just too quick.'

'So what happens to you?'

'Oh, I go too.' Margot rubbed his face in his hands. 'Aren't you going to come back to London with me? We can take a taxi from Hampton Wick.'

'All right,' Blanc agreed. 'But you still haven't told me why you're involved.'

'Surely it's easy to see. I'm fairly respectable, even if I do have the English complaint of the male species. No, I have friends who are influential. No one suspects the professional class after all. I'm sure you don't suspect your lawyer. What do you do?'

'I'm a teacher.' Margot didn't pursue it.

Blanc stood up and looked out of the carriage window again. The train had slowed down. 'So you'll be off in three weeks.'

'Yes. Thank God. But I really can't see myself bearing up under the strain.'

'You will, you will,' Blanc said.

The train pulled up at Hampton Wick. They got out of the carriage, and walked through the ticket hall. 'We're in luck, Dennis.' A taxi driver was asleep over his steering wheel. Margot rapped on the window.

'Parliament Hill, Hampstead, via Hyde Park Corner.'

'It'll be three quid.'

'All right.'

Margot dropped Blanc at Hyde Park Corner so he could walk back to 'his place in the West End'. 'I *can* trust you?' Margot said.

'Yes,' replied Blanc. 'Of course.'

Marcia woke Blanc late the next morning.

'You were lucky again, I hear,' she said.

'What do you mean, "I hear", what have you heard?'

'Margot arrived back at his flat in Hampstead at about three in the morning. Locked his door, at the same time locking in someone already there with him. He was stabbed to death, stabbed and strangled. His body had twenty-eight knife wounds in it.'

'When did you hear this?'

'This morning, an hour ago. McCall has asked me to get a report from you.'

'I wasn't there. Margot dropped me off at Hyde Park Corner and I came on here in another taxi.'

'No, McCall doesn't mean the murder, he wants to know what you said to each other. It's not the murder he's interested in.'

'Poor old Margot, if I'd known that was going to happen I might have been more generous.'

'What do you mean?'

'Never mind.'

10

'Try and remember everything Margot told you,' Marcia began slowly, 'all that he said about himself and the others.'

She sat on the bed in Blanc's room whilst he shaved.

'There's a chance he was bluffing, throwing you off the scent.'

'He couldn't have been. He didn't know I was on it. In any case I wasn't. All I had to do was drop the hearing device in his pocket.'

'Did you?'

'Of course not. It was a ridiculous idea, he'd have found it when he put his hand in his pocket to get his handkerchief, or whatever he kept in there. It was pointless.'

'All right then, so he picked you up.'

'It was coincidence, I just felt someone watching me from the opposite platform. The odds were against it, it could have been anyone. As it happened it was Margot. He came over and asked me my name so I told him it was Dennis; he asked me to take a ride, to Hampton Wick. So we got into the next train and he began to edge up to me. Quite honestly I didn't believe he was queer at all until he looked at me. "Dennis", he said, pleading. Then it was clear enough. He did say he wanted me to call him Clifford and not Cliff, he seemed to have a thing about it. Anyhow I stood up and later he asked me to sit down again next to him. The train had stopped at one of the stations on the way and when I looked down at Margot he was weeping. My rejection broke him.'

'Then ...'

'You don't want to hear all this.'

'I don't, but McCall does and I've got to tell him.'

'Well, then he said something about being involved, he said he was being blackmailed along with three others. I suppose he meant Donnelly, Ames and Waterman.'

'It could be true.'

'It makes sense.'

Blanc rubbed his face in his towel and dried his hands.

'Then he mentioned assassinations, something about three weeks and a flight to Canada. He said he couldn't stand it. He wouldn't tell me who's to be assassinated.'

Marcia got up from the bed, and handed Blanc his shirt.

'The sub-section doesn't know either.'

'Aren't we seeing McCall about this?' Blanc asked.

'No. He's away from London for a while. He's staying with his clergyman friend in Swindon. I'm doing the report on your meeting with Margot. Then I'll hand it to the sub-section. So McCall will see it when he gets back.'

This meant that Blanc probably wouldn't have to endure another lunch with McCall for a while at least. He bent down to do up his shoelaces.

'You know, Marcia, I think McCall's in trouble. Suppose he killed Margot. It might not have been Margot's own people who did it. But, if it was, then they'll have found out that Margot had already talked. But suppose McCall killed him— then he's got another murder enquiry to stop. Another approach to the police. That won't endear him to the Commissioner.'

'I don't think it was anything to do with McCall. The sub-section's sure the other side did it. They think they've most likely left the country already. Most likely they sent someone in from abroad to do it.'

Marcia looked out through the windows.

'You know,' Blanc said, 'I don't think any of this is properly planned. I just can't see why McCall had to kill the girl. I just don't understand what she had to do with this.'

Marcia wasn't listening.

'What will you do when it's over?' she asked eventually.

'Go home I expect.'

'But you can't.'

'By the time this is over things may have changed.'

'I doubt it. You killed a Russian didn't you?'

'Yes. But it may not be an indictable offence by the time I go back to Prague.'

Blanc realised he couldn't move. But the waiting was becoming intolerable. Why should he help the English?

So he waited. He had thought that McCall's people would act fast, without delay. How much easier, he thought, to have kept the old system; to give him the initiative—to 'send him in', 'give him a free hand', instead of locking him up in a businessmen's retreat.

He sat in a large well-sprung armchair in the corner of the Smoking Room. He had taken to going there after lunch and to watching the people walking past in St James's Square. A man spent most of his afternoon cleaning cars, dousing them with a tattered chamois leather which he dipped into a bright yellow bucket. From time to time Blanc would fall asleep.

He even regretted that Margot had gone. Mainly because Margot was a part of the venture he actually understood—a victim of blackmail like himself: homosexual maybe, but then beggars couldn't be choosers, except amongst their own kind. Margot's very personal failure made him human, at any rate in Blanc's eyes. Finally he couldn't pretend to be anything other than he was. When it came to it all he was looking for was friendship and at his age it wasn't all that easy to get. It was just bad luck that he'd got himself involved in the first place. Presumably somebody had chosen him for the Security Commission and if they had known more about him then it would have been easier to persuade him kindly against serving on it. But no one did. People would be shocked by the murder. His few acquaintances would wonder justifiably why it happened. The cavers in their Quarterly would read:

'We announce with much regret the death of Clifford Margot whose contribution to ... etc.'

Or the Old Boys' Bulletin of St Edward's School, Oxford:

'With regret we have learned of the death of Clifford Margot who will be remembered for ... etc.'

Or the Staff Magazine of the electronics company:

'Our representative in Paris, Bonn, Frankfurt and Washington, Mr Clifford Margot, died at home ... etc.'

But supposing they knew the truth: the solicitor's clerk,

political scandals, international intrigue and the threat of assassination? There was a point at which respectability made shock impossible. If you really thought about it, Margot could have been murdered by his own people. They simply could not stand this sort of traitor who betrayed the morals of a class. He was dead even before the knives went in.

It was a racket and fortunately for him Blanc felt it offered some protection because McCall couldn't jettison him at this stage. He was too valuable and a great deal of care had been taken to fit him precisely into the hierarchy so that he knew enough to do his job but not enough to be dangerous.

Nevertheless, underneath the hierarchy there was a bureaucratic structure hardening itself, and the harder it got the more likely it would be to crack—assuming that someone knew the right place to hammer. In spite of the pains McCall had taken to emphasise that no single person knew the right part to hit it could still be supposed that individuals were being done away with. After all, if you made the secrets impossible to steal, what was left? Intimidation and assassination. In many respects it had been no bad thing that secrets were so easy to trade in.

So McCall's suggestion that there was a double agent didn't quite make sense, unless he was operating at a very low level, say directly against Blanc. What was more to the point was *who would get shot?*

'Tea and toast.'

Blanc looked out over St James's Square and watched a woman backing a long green car into a parking bay.

'Tea and toast....' A white jacketed waiter stood at the side of his chair. He wasn't asking if he wanted tea and toast. He was just announcing it.

The tea was horribly the same. The toast without its crust. Nothing to chew on, the tea weak, no leaves; four wet lumps of sugar in the saucer.

Blanc gazed out of the tall windows again at the trees in the square.

The wind was stripping them of their leaves and the decay of autumn was being cleared up.

He thought again of McCall. Why had he been so on edge?

The streak of anarchy was crystallising in Blanc—he was deriving pleasure from seeking McCall's break-down. McCall was authority. A well-oiled machine issuing orders, directing operations. There were no principles, no ideals, just rules and a certain amount of sentimentality about the past. One's university, regiment, club, one's this and that.

The game was played because of the rules not in spite of them. You fitted the game to the rules. A hard twist to follow, but it was that which led Blanc to think that McCall might even be a double agent. Look at the facts.

McCall was a buffer between Blanc, Helmsman and the collection of information. It was McCall who'd recruited him, who from the very start had arranged for Cairns to watch him from Cambridge. It could be a classic, pure double bluff. McCall had placed someone in between himself and the other side so that his chiefs would think he was more than ever eager to penetrate the others.

McCall had trained Blanc himself with Smith. They had briefed him and given him the orders.

The murder of Jean Mungo was intended simply as a threat. Similar in kind to the beating up in the tube. Neither of the events could have meant anything else.

Blanc drank his tea and by now the sugar had dissolved into a sticky stream in the saucer. He turned away from the window.

There were a number of elderly men receiving tea from the waiter's silverplated tray.

And there was a clanking of spoons against cups.

Blanc felt acutely at odds with the stiff old men. He tried to listen to a conversation two of them were having.

'Let them determine their own futures ...'

'Quite. Can't interfere ...'

'They don't with us. Why should we with them?'

'Can't afford it ...'

The two men sipped their tea loudly.

'Hot.'

'Hot.'

Blanc stood up and turned his chair round again with irritation. The toast was too soggy to eat. He walked to the centre of the room and took a magazine from a circular table.

He looked at pictures of society weddings, an article on a country estate in Rutland, a military parade and a blurred full-page photograph of a large-nosed girl with blond hair swept sternly up on the top of her head, reminding him of nothing so much as a ship.

McCall a double agent.

The subtlest way to avert suspicion was to suggest that there was a double agent, not to name him, not even to hint at a name; just mention the possibility in passing, indirectly and almost light-heartedly; and if one was particularly daring one would say 'And anyone could be a double agent.' McCall would scratch his palms in thought and would lift himself up beyond suspicion; cunning and idealism simply did not work well together. Think of it the other way round, suppose that they *had* to work together for a time, that McCall was an unwilling double agent. This explained his tension, his edginess.

It had become dark outside in the square, and Blanc had not noticed that the lights in the Smoking Room had been turned on. McCall a double agent. There was a fifty-fifty chance, it wasn't what you said that mattered, it was what you didn't say.

The two sides were evenly matched, in some respects they looked alike, even down to the raised stitching of their gently tailored suits: he recalled Donnelly standing by the porter's desk. Impeccable. And McCall; he too would have been impeccable, indistinguishable in the Royal Services Club. There was no drabness about espionage, drabness was obvious.

And flamboyance, romance, the scented breast handkerchief, and faded rose—that was fiction. What mattered was the reality of uniformity, and the hidden discipline of plainness. Men should not just blend into the background, they *were* the background. It was almost an aesthetic with its own structure for discourse: don't argue with the obvious precepts about central issues; argue from an oblique stand-point and withdraw in another direction. So never, as it were, leave by the door you came in through, make them think you left by the back door; when, in fact, you left by the window—on the first floor.

This approach would suit McCall. If you made your task more difficult than it was no one would think of you as a traitor. If you drove yourself to the limits of hard work and appeared overtired no one would seek to question its morality. In espionage the more you committed yourself the freer you were.

McCall had been quite right at the farmhouse. He had said that it was a four-dimensional jig-saw, that the bits had to fit top and bottom as well as sideways and even then had to fit in with *something else*. (It was a difficult idea to understand.) Blanc was drawing nearer. The *something else* was the English professional class. Admirable and respectable, founded on tradition that is indefinable and hardly related to practicality.

One man was sitting alone, a professional man—newly acceded to the class, newly classified, so to speak; one man sat alone to his right. Blanc had slumped down in the deep chair and watched this fat man sitting at an oblique angle to him. The waiter approached him and stood a few paces away from the fat man's chair. His arms dangled at his sides, the fingers of his left hand holding the rim of the silver-plated tray.

'Campari,' the fat man said.

'With soda, sir?'

'Please. And have the evenin' papers come in?' He did not pronounce the 'g'—'evenin',' he said. Blanc realised that he too was noticing the aberration.

The fat man's dry blond hair fell thinly over his forehead and he had disquieting reddish tufts on his cheeks. It was a putty-like face, it had an infantile teasing sexuality about it: the promise of a gay, sharp energy. He had a square black brief case packed with papers on his knees, and as he shut it he caught and bent the edges of a thin journal. (You weren't supposed to bring business into the Smoking Room, brief cases weren't allowed.) The fat man had broken the rules. Blanc waited for him to be reprimanded. But he wasn't. The red Campari was brought to him and Blanc noticed that the fat man left the change on the silver tray. You weren't allowed to do that either.

106

Rules should be kept.

But if you were an old member they could be waived, the certainty of trust had to be established, ultimately you were acceptable even if you couldn't say your 'g's'. It was style that counted and you could be stylish when your trust was established by mutual, silent arrangement. The unspoken trust of servant and master which bred the suspicion of outsiders.

Blanc despised it, an act of defiance was needed. Perhaps he should walk past the fat man and nudge the sticky Campari off the arm of the chair and stain his trouser front. Humiliate the fat man, make him utterly laughable.

He couldn't do it, it would be conspicuous.

Perhaps the little man needed love, like Margot—not the same sort, but a mother love, dominating. Maybe he could get it from McCall; McCall—man-of-action, who was immediately admirable. The fat man's untrained intellect would admire its opposite in McCall, it well fitted the intense love affairs that lesser intellectuals had from afar with a man of action. And when the two poles were reconciled at last someone magical arose—a twentieth-century hero, a laurelled politician or poet-soldier.

Blanc was bored. The waiting had given him time to think again, to search for reasons and proof. He still needed the confines of the British Museum to sort them out in. A London men's club was wrong mainly because it was incurably frustrating. So were his suspicions of McCall's deception, founded as they were upon his notion that McCall was in such an impregnable position from which to plot betrayal.

And Blanc would gain nothing whilst at the same time standing to lose everything.

God knew when Busek would strike. He wouldn't let him off the hook. Not now. A KGB warrant for his arrest doubled with the information he had about British Intelligence. Blanc was a political diamond. Universal currency.

And Marcia. She too would be lost if it all went wrong. Whatever happened he did not want to lose the possibility of loving her. It was right that they should love each other. It would outrage this club, it would batter its respectability, its cynicism and understatement.

Above all he could confound the professional classes, over-turn their values, beat up their hybrid tribalism.

Satisfied with his polemics he decided to capture the initiative.

Outside it was very cold. Snow could not be far off.

11

The Victorian church of St Margaret in Kensington ended a terrace which its inhabitants described as smart. The house fronts were painted in pastel greens, pinks and whites; so pale that Blanc was reminded of bars of soap. The church had been well preserved because the residents of the neighbourhood knew the value of nice appearances.

Their charity had crossed their doorsteps to the church lawn which had recently been mown for the last time that winter. Just in time before the snow. Someone had planted a trim row of cherry trees in long beds by the walls. In spring their bright flake blossoms would match the pastel house fronts. The slender trees had been strapped to raw wood supports that stood guard like sentries behind the railings which Blanc was leaning against.

A green partition door was half open in the porch. He listened to the last hymn of Matins. Only the women in the congregation seemed to be singing it:

'... Surely his goodness and mercy shall
   daily attend thee;
    Ponder anew
    What the Almighty can do
If to the end He befriend thee.'

They spat out the capitals and there was a long choral amen.

He crossed the road with a hand in his pocket turning over the flat hearing device. He let his forefinger rest on the priming switch.

About twenty people left the church in twos and threes. An elderly woman was bent double in a wheel chair. She jerked forward in it as her young companion tipped it slightly backwards up onto the pavement.

He saw the priest standing inside the porch—just his white cotton robes but not his face.

'Thank you, Father.'

'Good mornin'.' The priest nodded.

As Blanc recognised the missing 'g's the priest turned. Once more Blanc saw the cherubic face of Donald Ames whose outward signs of class had changed now that he was shrouded in a priestly billowing garb. He reminded Blanc of the giant eye-level advertisements in the underground depicting babies. When they caught him unawares they assumed a nightmarish quality of grotesque deformity.

He stared at this diminutive little man imparting warm gentleness to his bleak congregation.

The faithful lingered over their departures.

As the last of them left the church Ames walked along the pathway to the church gates: he had noticed Blanc staring at him from the other side of the road. Blanc was caught and looked at him awkwardly.

'Could I have a talk with you ... if you're free?'

'I'm sorry. Come back later would you, people are coming to the vicarage.' Ames was abrupt. But it was the chance Blanc had hoped for.

'Perhaps I could walk over to the vicarage with you?'

'All right. Come and have a sherry.'

For the first time in the whole business Blanc felt excited. He had taken the initiative himself. Ames would be easy.

'Good. Let's hurry and we can have a few minutes before they arrive. Let me just change out of this.'

Blanc read the titles of the literature displayed in the porch; ill-designed pamphlets. *Missions in Africa, Christian Marriage Today, Christianity and the Businessman.*

Ames was scurrying back down the aisle.

'Right,' he said. 'We can talk on the way. The vicarage is just over the road.' He waved an arm in front of him. 'And I'm afraid I've only got sherry.'

As he spoke Ames leaned close to Blanc's face in simulation of directness, but Blanc could smell the Vicar's nervous breath which was stale from public performance.

'Didn't see you in the service.'

'I arrived late.'

'In fact I don't think I've seen you here before at all. Or have I?'

'No. I've come just to see you. I'm trying to find some cousins. Fallon. John and Gay Fallon.'

'I don't think I can help.'

'But they used to go to church regularly.'

'That doesn't mean much. They might not have come here. Anyhow this area's a dormitory, people come and go all the time. Bed-sitters. I'm awfully bad at names.'

Ames led Blanc through his front door.

'I'll get some glasses,' he said. 'Find yourself a chair. I'll take my coat off.'

Like many men living on their own Ames always told himself what he was going to do before he did it. Blanc stood in the drawing-room, fingered the device and listened.

'Just getting a tray.'

Blanc wondered what the sub-section would make of someone who talked to himself.

'You haven't told me your name,' Ames called out.

'Blanc.'

'Ah. I thought perhaps it was Fallon.'

'No. It's not.'

'Quite. They were your relations, weren't they?'

'Yes. My mother's.'

Blanc looked around the room. The desk looked a likely place. But that was where Donnelly's was. Perhaps the window sill, under a chair, behind a picture.

Ames was calling again.

'There's nothing I can do for you Mr Blanc. You might try the Town Hall. Or the Library.'

Blanc could see Ames through the door. The device was in his hand.

Under the table. The telephone. The sideboard.

'Perhaps they'd help you. Only sorry I can't.'

Then Ames came in.

'Your face looks very familiar Mr Blanc. But then one sees so many.'

'I suppose you do.'

Ames took the glasses off a long rectangular tray and filled them with sherry.

They drank in silence. Ames didn't want to prolong the meeting. He was hurrying. And Blanc couldn't think of a move to delay him.

'There we are,' Ames said, putting down his glass.

Blanc stood up. But directly he did so Ames looked him in the eyes and then led him to the door.

'After you.'

'Thanks.'

'I'm sorry we haven't got anywhere.'

Outside Blanc realised he'd failed. He should have attached the device as soon as he could. Delay had lost him his opportunity.

If he met Ames again at the Royal Services Club it would be embarrassing—the coincidence might be hard to explain away.

The streets in Kensington were empty. The residents were having the Sunday lunches they always had.

A bus from Kensington swayed around Hyde Park Corner. A group of pigeons scattered themselves upwards to a lowering sky. The wind had dropped already as the snow began to fall. First it touched the tops of walls. Then, imperceptibly, it covered everything to grey and white. The sky had more in it to come.

He watched the transformation and didn't notice a taxi turn off towards Victoria.

It was a dull and white midday.

The solitary taxi fare stroked his wispy hair anxiously and pushed his thick gold-rimmed glasses up the bridge of his nose.

Cyril Barnes asked the driver to hurry.

12

Blanc had agreed to telephone Marcia at two in the afternoon when he returned to the Club. She had given him the number of a small restaurant in Chelsea which was enjoying a certain vogue as a meeting place on Sundays for West Indian singers and dancers. He was used to the dark corridor by now, he even ignored the staleness which had irritated him before.

His room was just as he had left it: a pile of Sunday newspapers thrown on his unmade bed, the washtowel had fallen from the rail under the basin and dropped into the waste-paper basket. As he retrieved it and replaced it on a hook in the wall he noticed an envelope on the chest of drawers. He read Marcia's large handwriting. *Meet you here at 3 Marcia*. He had told her the night before that he intended to spend Sunday morning alone; he would go for a drink in Kensington and spend the afternoon in the Club's library, which was always empty on Sundays. He had conceived the plan for contacting Ames on his own, and he had kept it to himself because it was a part of his intention to speed things up. No one could complain about that. Now he regretted that he hadn't been drinking after all.

It was not until four that Marcia knocked heavily on his door.

'How was your lunch?'

She was panting slightly. She had been running and her hair was awry.

'I haven't had any,' she said, 'McCall wanted to see me.'

'Why didn't you get him to take you?'

'Because Barnes phoned him and said you'd met Ames.'

'I didn't see him,' Blanc said. 'Was it *Cyril* Barnes? I didn't see him.'

'You wouldn't have done, he was following you.'

He noticed that Marcia seemed to have been crying—her eyelids were red, the blood vessels on her forehead stood out. He had never seen her angry : 'You were with him two hours ago. This is what McCall's been waiting for, a mistake, a step out of line. He thought you'd make it and Barnes was there to see it.'

Her eyes were full of tears.

'You've been overdoing it.'

She showed no interest in his sympathy. 'You'd better tell McCall you didn't see Ames. You can face him yourself.'

'I haven't got to *face* anyone, let alone McCall.'

'Once Barnes gets his nails in he doesn't let go.'

She was shaking.

Undoing her overcoat she breathed deeply, as if her crying had tired her out.

'Believe me. I know how they've dealt with people like you in the past.'

'Who for instance?'

'No names. There never are. People who don't have friends and aren't in telephone directories. They don't have parentages. It's the wanderers they go for. The émigrés like you who have too much to lose, who really value their refuge here, who become more English than the English.'

'You think that's me I suppose.'

'Yes. Sometimes they bob up again like tealeaves. But they always sink. Have you ever watched tealeaves sink?' Marcia asked him.

'No.'

'Well you should. You'd learn something about yourself.'

Marcia was distraught. She was sharing his fate and she knew that McCall acted on suspicion. He couldn't afford not to.

'O.K. then, what do I do?'

'Just *tell* McCall why you went to Ames's place, and just remember that there's a scare on about a double agent. The first people they vet are the free-lancers, and they don't *try* you; you do just get disposed of, a body washed up, a suicide,

114

a car accident and the emergency operation by a chosen surgeon. Official murder's easy. So tell McCall. Tell him everything.' She was pleading. 'If the flag goes up that there's really a double agent loose it gets vicious, believe me, really vicious. Each time it's happened so far they just eliminated the possibilities.'

They talked for longer than they should have done: Marcia remembered after an hour or so, that McCall wanted Blanc at his headquarters. Yes, even though it was Sunday. 'Go out. And bloody well get him,' McCall had told her. 'Now.' He had made her cry. She felt lonely and frightened. They wanted Blanc, he was under suspicion and no one was given the benefit of the doubt. Loyalties in the new system had not proved strong; in the old days the men on the ground stood out against the bureaucracy and the officialdom, even the idea of ranks for personnel; but now there was the computer to rage against. So the executive had been ruthless, they had cut back and cut out savagely. They had tried to keep it from most of the free-lance agents, the recruits. But it was impossible, even the staff of the sub-section talked.

The snow blew around their shoes as they walked to Pall Mall. There they took a taxi to Victoria and once there the policeman on duty gave them each a round badge with a number in the centre.

He spoke on the telephone and a straight-backed man appeared from across the hall.

'Sixth floor staff please. Then Room 10.'

The lift doors opened.

'Left please.'

Blanc was shown into an office on his own and looked wanly at Marcia as he went. Two strips of fluorescent lighting fixed precariously to the ceiling, making the pale blue walls even colder. The room was stale with the smell of cigarettes and very warm.

He wished he hadn't been to Ames's house or even the tidy snobbish little church. So there was a double agent. But then he himself knew only a few of the people involved. Maybe it was someone else. Someone whose mission would be changed half-way through to meet someone at a rendezvous quite innocently.

There would be a bullet in the back.

A body would fall kicking in its death and a quiet man, a professional, would leave quietly and not by the route he had come.

Why should he tell McCall he had been to Ames's place?

Fear caught up with him. What Marcia had been trying to tell him was that he was under suspicion. And that was why he had been brought to Victoria on a Sunday evening by a woman he wanted very badly.

It was never explained to him why he was made to wait on his own for so long. This interval in his employment was no break, but an overture to questioning, maybe to interrogation—there was a difference obvious to the staff. The pale blue room was soundproofed to provide some monstrous silence for contemplation of sins against the realm. There was of course no God to turn to for succour in the waiting moments before confession, no majestic stained glass to depict gentle apostles, no clear coloured arrangement of the green fields of paradise. Neither was there an infusion of winter light to tame the blue paint of government waiting-rooms.

No one remembered to put a window in the wall. One was not left alone to face the priest and father with an untidy conscience, one knew no guilt because there was no crime. It was a softening of the mind; the mind its own drug forcing humiliation upon itself in front of striped suits, white stiff collars, the tailor's label in the wallet pocket, the well-shined brogues; the *pleasantness* of an English Sunday evening.

Blanc's weakness was becoming clearer to him; he sat outside the unformed ideologies of internal and external security which belonged to the established manners of men of convenient class. Convenient because the spies, the agents, were bred of a class which balanced itself between the aristocracy and middle-classes—just above the reliability of the parson, stockbroker, lawyer or doctor.

Men and women who were 'something' in the Foreign Office. It was a definition of type, not birth because now there were men from British grammar schools or who had 'transferred' from other offices dealing with emergent African states. Who on earth spied for the Africans? He remembered that the game was multidimensional, the jig-saw puzzle you build up like some grandiose Meccano crane, and the safety of professional men depended upon its strength. Strength lay in complexity and finally it was complexity of manners that gave the professional man his security.

Blanc felt he was caught simply because he knew his weaknesses and couldn't overcome them. He knew he had the ability to see the abstractions of government security but he couldn't manage their translation into practical terms.

He was torn by fear and divided between his dread of Busek and the outstanding debts he owed to some notion of national preservation. He felt deeply unsure of himself.

Sitting back from the table and its surface of shiny mahogany he pressed his finger tips against its edge. With a nail of his right hand he dug a deep line beneath the table top. He joined it up unwittingly with a line that someone else had made before him, someone else waiting in awe of the authority of the system.

He reconstructed his visit to Ames; remembering as far as he was able the times, the faces he had seen, the invalid and her young nurse, the number of the bus he had taken to Piccadilly.

He thought of the priest.

It was now evening and Ames would be taking evensong. He might still be thinking of Mr Blanc. He took his mind off it and thought instead of his flat, which would be getting damp. He wondered whether the Wardour Street rats had found a way in from the underground network of runs beneath Soho. He recalled a prostitute in St Anne's Court called Judy who had gone mad and was found feeding a family of rats in an old shoe box. The story told in the cafés was that the police and welfare officers had quarrelled. No one wanted to remove mad Judy. In the end six men took her struggling to an ambulance; one of them carried down three suitcases and dumped them on a pile of garbage in Berwick Street. The three girls who sold themselves in Judy's basement rummaged in the heap and took away four horse-whips and a full-length garment like an airman's suit but made of leather. The peroxide had begun to destroy Judy's hair and as they carried her to the ambulance she yelled out 'Stop them, pigs, pigs, pigs. ...' Blanc often wondered what secrets she would reveal in her madness.

'I'm a little disappointed,' McCall began, as if he had rehearsed his opening, 'that you've let us down.'

He sat behind a desk. The office was small: a map of Europe was spread out in a low chair in the corner.

'Perhaps we briefed you too well, it's happened before.'

'You hardly briefed me at all, you know that.'

'We might not have *trained* you. But we briefed you very thoroughly indeed. You can't deny that. Even so you were misguided to confide in Ames.'

'But I did not confide in him.'

'Barnes has a very different story to tell.'

'Which is what?'

McCall didn't reply, instead he just lifted his telephone. 'Would you ask Barnes to come in. ...' He replaced the receiver slowly. 'We'll see what he has to say.'

The telephone rang.

'Ring back would you. Who is it?'

McCall listened. Blanc noticed the same twitch above the eye he'd seen in the restaurant once before.

'I see,' he said. 'Who last saw him? Where?'

He listened again without interrupting the person on the other end.

'We'll send someone out. Now. And you're quite sure he hasn't waited?' He put the receiver down and pushed the telephone to the side of the desk.

'Barnes hasn't waited.' McCall had paled.

'Aren't you going to tell me what he said?'

'Barnes had been told to follow you at any time you left the Club. Unless you were going out on instructions. He saw you leave for Ames's place, saw you wait outside the church and then go with him to Ames's house. And you went in with him, didn't you?'

'Yes.'

118

'You tell me why.'

'I took a device to plant on him. I've already told Marcia Helmsman. All right, so I never got a chance to plant it. I couldn't have done it without Ames noticing.'

'I know there's no device there. But why did you go in the first place?'

'That's what my job is. Isn't it? To plant the devices. O.K. So I failed.'

'That's not the point. Why did you go without instructions?'

'Because I wanted to speed it up. It seemed a good time.'

'That isn't a reason.'

'It's the only one I've got.'

McCall pointed to some notes on a quarto piece of paper in front of him. He said, 'That isn't Barnes's version.'

'So?'

'Unfortunately he isn't here to tell it to you himself. When he saw you go into the vicarage with Ames he broke in at the back of the house. He heard everything that was said.'

'And what did he hear?'

'He heard you tell Ames to leave the country. That the sub-section was closing in on him and Donnelly and Waterman. That there was enough evidence against Donnelly to send him to jail for thirty years and that there soon would be against him too.'

'And what did Barnes hear Ames say?'

'That he had unfinished business but would take heed of what you told him....'

'Do you believe this?' Blanc asked.

'There's no reason why I shouldn't.'

Blanc stood up. 'There's every bloody reason. It's pure invention.' Blanc was furious. 'Either you're thick skinned or thick headed....'

'It won't help you ...'

'Come on, McCall. Barnes is taking you for a ride. Can't you see it?'

They were both standing.

'It's your word against Barnes's,' McCall said.

His silence was accusing.

Blanc could hear the muffled sounds of the traffic outside. The snow changed everything. Even the sounds of London seemed deeper. The car horns droned, a police bell rang somewhere down below like a muffled alarm clock.

McCall rubbed the side of his face and looked hard at Blanc. He half smiled.

'Sit down.'

'What are you going to do about it?' asked Blanc.

'Find Barnes. You see as it happens there isn't a back entrance to Ames's place. There again, I needed to be sure. So you made a mistake in going to Ames's place. But at least it means we've got Barnes.'

Blanc didn't reply. Instead he felt sick.

McCall sat down behind his desk and adjusted the blotting paper with the tips of his fingers.

Now he would see that Blanc was softened.

'So what have you got to tell about Ames?'

'Nothing. Except that he can't say his "g's".'

Blanc realised that McCall already knew all he wanted to about Ames and probably about Barnes as well. After all he rarely asked questions to which he didn't know the answers.

And Blanc could see the inconsistencies in Cyril Barnes, who had really been interested in him and not in the translation of Boehme. Barnes had got the translator's initials wrong—he had called him D. G. Barker. Blanc didn't bother to point out the difference to McCall. He was annoyed that he hadn't given more thought to C. J. Barker because no Boehme expert would ever get the initials wrong. He told himself he shouldn't imagine so much, that he shouldn't allow the waiting to make him paranoid.

'What are you going to do about Barnes?'

'That's my affair,' McCall said abruptly. 'Let's look at how far you've got. There's less time than you seem to think. Donnelly and Margot have been accounted for in their different ways and I'm not sure we've even got to worry about Ames. But Margot knew the targets for assassination, at least we think he did. That may explain why they did him in. He'd been getting too flirtatious, he was a risk.'

McCall paused, looking him hard in the eyes. 'Anyway, all you've got to do now is what you're told.'

Revealing his secrets meant for McCall something akin

120

to another man losing his potency. The pleasure in his work, if there was any, derived from his easy access to secret information and indeed the manipulation of it.

When he told Blanc that he was to do what he was told he was of course embarking on a briefing.

They were going to go ahead, irrespective of Barnes.

Apparently the meeting place of Donnelly and his associates in the Royal Services Club was in its disused basement. If nothing else, this explained why McCall had insisted that he study the plans of the cellars when, as he put it, 'they were in the country together'.

McCall leaned forward on his desk and tried to balance a pencil on its end.

'We've got two devices in the room Donnelly uses for meetings,' he said, 'but all we've had is silence. Which is why we suspected the room was a cover. Smith reread the minutes of all the club's committee meetings. Anyone could have seen how it was set up: Donnelly was elected to the committee in 1962, and he was given the post of adviser to the Steward. That meant he was supposed to interest himself in the club's catering facilities. And after two years wastage was cut by half. The committee was very pleased. Then, a few months later, in January of 1966, some extensive pilfering started. As a result Donnelly sacked six of the kitchen staff.'

McCall was turning over a memorandum. He paused to scan its pages and continued:

'Only Donnelly's persistent support of several junior staff members averted some kind of strike. So he therefore managed to gain the confidence of the staff, of the rest of the committee and of the decrepit members who cared to interest themselves in the whole business.'

McCall produced a plan attached to a different memorandum. 'No one,' he continued, 'questioned the reconstruction of the basement as a store. A temporary partition was built.'

He showed Blanc the plan. 'Beyond that the place was left to the vermin.'

'Where do you want the device planted?' Blanc asked.

McCall indicated the area beyond the partition.

'Just fix it in there. As soon as you can. Some time tomorrow night.'

'And Waterman?'

'I've told my chiefs that we won't ask you to see him. There's no point. Maybe we can deal with him ourselves.'

'So that's it. It concludes the job....'

'Yes. As far as I can see.'

'Are you arranging the payments?'

'Someone here will do that. You'll get quite a sum, half a year's salary at Grade 14. Something like four and a half thousand.'

'Is that all?'

'It's not bad. And there will be some additional cash payments to see you through until Busek is dealt with.'

'And you are doing that *personally*?'

'Yes. No one else can. It's an informal arrangement.'

'When do I hear if it's confirmed?'

'That depends on when I arrange it.'

13

It was well after midnight and bitterly cold when Blanc and Marcia left the administration headquarters in Victoria.

As they walked to the station to find a taxi Marcia put her arm through Blanc's and they picked their way carefully over the freezing snow. 'So what do you think of McCall?' she asked once Blanc had explained the curious interview.

'I don't know,' he said, 'I don't know. His currency is such a mixture of truth and lies that I'm beginning to wonder if he isn't deceiving himself. Someone must think he's reliable. I suppose that on balance I've got more time for him than Barnes.'

Marcia frowned. 'I don't know why Barnes should have said it.'

'Neither do I. Sowing confusion perhaps.'

'Was he angry about Ames?'

'There wasn't anything to be angry about.'

'So what's he going to do?'

'He said he'd leave it. I don't believe him though.'

'So maybe he does trust you.'

'He's got to. He may just have been fishing for something. The bit about Barnes may have been a bluff. I expect he's checking everyone. He'll have to hurry if what he said about Donnelly's time running out is true.'

They waited under the canopy of the station. Marcia stood close to him. 'There may have been another reason for trying you out,' she said.

'Such as?'

'He asked me this morning if I was in love with you.'

'And what did you say?'

'I said I was.'

'You've never told me....'

'I have.'

'Not me. You've told McCall.'

She half smiled at him. 'Sorry.'

'There's no need to apologise. And I don't believe you.'

She put her arms round his shoulders, and looked up at him.

'I think you're frightened. Scared perhaps. Of tomorrow night.'

'Of course I am. It's the end of all this and I just want to get it finished off properly.'

In the taxi on the way back to St James's Marcia reached forward to the glass partition and closed the small shutter.

'There's something else. McCall never told you what that room's being used for.'

Blanc looked at her curiously. 'It's just a meeting place. It was bloody silly of McCall to think that they'd use the other rooms.'

'He had to make sure of you. Just think back to why he called me in there this morning. He had a suspicion. He reckoned that you'd have told me....'

Blanc interrupted her. 'It's more likely ...' he paused, 'that he was trying to scare me into finishing things off on my own accord.'

Marcia shook her head. 'You're too charitable. The point is that McCall never told you that the basement is being used as a store.'

'But he did.' Blanc said.

'Yes, but the partition wall at the end of the food store disguises the entrance to a room beyond. And that's the interesting one. That's where Donnelly's people meet. And that's where they've stored their weapons. They've been smuggled in there during the last four months, just small arms and ammunition. But enough for their purposes. I don't understand why McCall never told you. Particularly if you're going down there tomorrow night. You're bound to see the stuff. And if anything goes wrong and someone's there they may quite easily try some of it out.'

The taxi driver pulled down the shutter.

'Where do you want?'

Blanc leaned forward on his seat.

124

'The other side of the square.'

As he sat back Marcia took his hand gently in hers.

Blanc paid the driver and he and Marcia stood alone on the pavement outside the club.

'I wonder,' Blanc said, 'whether McCall's a liar. Whether he knows perfectly well who the double agent is and that it's not Barnes. I just wonder how much of this is a bluff.'

Marcia didn't reply immediately. She followed Blanc's eyes. He was watching the snow-laden sky.

Then Blanc said, 'McCall does a conjuring trick and has you wondering how he does it. But I think that he's using one conjuring trick to disguise another.'

'I don't care too much,' she said. 'It won't affect us.'

'I wouldn't bank on that.'

She knocked on Blanc's door the following night at about ten minutes before midnight.

Blanc had spent the day walking. In the morning he had gone to Kensington Park Gardens. They were covered in snow. A man in a dark blue overcoat had been fussing around a small boy who was trying unsuccessfully to launch a model yacht on the boating pond. It was a bright, cold morning with only a slight wind; eventually a small breeze caught the sails and the yacht made its way slowly and in state across the pond between bits of ice. Immediately the little boy and the man, presumably his father, set off running as fast as they could around the edge of the pond. Before they had got half-way round the boy tripped and fell. He burst into tears and howled loudly. His father came back, picked him up in his arms and looked across at Blanc as if to say mind your own business. Blanc looked away embarrassed.

He watched the staff of the London Museum going through the entrance.

'Ah,' said a man wearing thick-lensed glasses.

'Ah,' the girl replied mockingly. The cold air had made her cheeks shine. 'Ah John,' she said again and they laughed.

Blanc envied them the quiet warm retreat of the museum and thought of the British Museum, and then of Marcia. He felt elated, and wondered when and how he could ask her to marry him and then thought he was being childish.

It had been very cold, and early in the afternoon the sky seemed to lower once more, closing London in with a grey and freezing blanket. Headlines on the newsstands were heavy and black: SNOW PARALYSIS IN MIDLANDS and STANDARD FORECAST: FREEZING SNOW HAZARD. But during the evening it became a little warmer and by nine o'clock the snow began to fall once more.

'It looks like Moscow,' Marcia said.

'You've never seen it, you'd stand out in it anyway. And I don't mind if I never see it.'

'With your white face it'll be easier for you to hide. Actually it's grey so you'll be better off in slush. Let's have a look at the device, the one you were going to leave for Ames.'

Blanc took the small container from a drawer and handed it to her.

'What time are you going down?'

'I'll have to wait until the porter's finished his rounds. When he gets back to his desk.'

'I'll come with you.'

'It'd be pointless.'

'How long will it take, twenty minutes maybe? I'll come too.'

'There's no point, Marcia.'

'Here, take this,' she held out a small pencil torch.

It had not occurred to Blanc that the cellars might have no lights.

The front staircase of the Royal Services Club was an extravagant construction and thickly carpeted.

On the first floor it joined a wide balcony and from this Blanc could see the porter's desk. He would have a clear view of him when he returned.

He stood back against the wall in darkness. All the main lights in the hallway had been turned off, but a small desk light was still on behind the porter's desk. Blanc waited. Somewhere on the ground floor a door shut. He heard a faint whistling; some army tune, a march.

Then it was quiet again. The porter must have gone into

the main bar directly beneath, for eventually he heard the bar door being locked and the porter's keys jingling. He saw the blue-suited porter strut across the hallway, lift a section of the counter in front of the desk and disappear behind it.

Blanc went down the staircase, the carpet dulling his footsteps. When he reached the bottom he stopped and looked across to the desk. The porter was sitting with his back to him. He had heard nothing. Blanc turned down the passageway.

He walked quickly across the dining-room. No one had drawn the curtains and the snow in the square outside lit the tall room with an even bluish light.

He pushed his way through the swing doors to the kitchens and held onto them letting them swing back gently. A row of ovens at eye level lined the wall opposite him and he could just make out a doorway leading to the steps which would take him to the basement. Here it would be safe to turn on the lights.

He looked down the stairs and, leaning out into the dark, felt up and down the wall for a light switch. But he couldn't find one and cursed the almost useless beam of the little torch.

He edged his way across to the other side of the doorway, surprised it was so wide. He felt up and down the wall and eventually his hand bumped a round metallic switch, an old-fashioned kind, round and raised up from the wall on a small wooden block. He peered behind him and stood still before switching on the light. The silence was oppressive.

He flicked the switch, again he waited, but no light went on. The bulb must have blown.

The plans, he remembered, had shown a deep flight of stairs descending into a basement passage: if he could edge his way down the stairs he would find two doors opposite, one leading to an old coal hole long since closed off, the other into the store room.

He began to half feel his way down the stairs. There seemed to be far more than he had expected. Occasionally they creaked and each time the silence was broken he stopped and listened.

He reached the bottom of the stairs and looked up.

But there was no light to help him.

He groped forward again, found the door to the coal hole and then, moving to his left, he found the door to the store room. The doorhandle was lower than he had expected, on the left hand side, but he realised that it would be locked; it surprised him when he found that the handle had jammed and that although the door was closed it was not in fact properly shut. Surely the kitchen people would normally keep it locked?

He pulled the door open and then shut it behind him. Still he could see nothing. He tried to remember the plans and wondered if they had been revised to show the whereabouts of the door in the partition at the end of the room.

Again he wondered why the door was open; he stood quite still.

If only he had a proper light.

He tried to find a switch but there didn't seem to be one. He decided to set off like a blind man, with arms outstretched, his feet a little in front of him. He reckoned that he had some twenty-five or thirty feet to go. He began to make his way across. After half a dozen steps he hit a pile of cardboard cartons which had been stacked up to the level of his chest, but worked his way along them and imagined that he had covered half the distance. Once again he bumped into something, maybe a wooden crate, and reaching down he felt only bottles. He was almost there, when his fingers touched a dry brick wall. He thought that he had probably crossed the room at an angle and would be near the far left corner of it, so he worked his way along the wall and after ten feet he felt the partition; beyond this would be the void, Donnelly's meeting room. He pressed his palms against the partition and it slid uneasily to one side. Why was it unlocked?

The partition was heavy; on the other side of it was a metal door, with no edges to work a knife into—whoever built it had done a good job. Half-way down it, at about waist level, was the lock covered by a small flap, which Blanc was able to hold between his thumb and forefinger, and he pulled hard on it. The door opened and he slid the partition door shut behind him.

128

It was the smell that surprised him: the stench of putrefaction, stale food and rotting meat.

The room was full of it.

He lifted his hand to his mouth. He thought at first that food had been left to decompose in there and rats had taken over.

He found a light switch. This one worked. The room was much longer than he had supposed. It was divided into low alcoves at the other side, which perhaps used to house ovens or something years ago. It was chaotic: upturned crates with their packing strewn all over the floor; a green filing cabinet on its side, its drawers hanging out, paper strewn about—and everywhere the terrible smell. Blanc's first reaction was to retreat, simply to get out and leave this dirty underbelly of the club.

The smell was foul and twice he almost retched.

There seemed no point in fixing the device because even if Donnelly had been there Blanc didn't believe that he would be coming back.

His eyes were stinging: smells always went to his eyes.

He kicked a cardboard box and packing straw slid out of it.

As he was deciding whether or not to leave, as if in a waking nightmare, he realised someone was in there with him.

And he was right.

It was only a whimper. Someone was calling his name.

He walked over more packing cases to the alcoves at the far end and saw Cyril Barnes. He lay on his back with his legs crossed awkwardly. His temples were covered in thick streams of blood and he was making desperate attempts to lick it out of his mouth.

He began to pant.

Blanc leaned over him and putting his hand behind Barnes' neck he tried to lift his head. Barnes coughed feebly.

Blanc looked round for something to prop him up with. Lying next to Barnes was a three-quarter-length coat, the very same coat that he had seen before in the Piccadilly underground.

Barnes seemed to be trying to say something.

Very slowly Barnes said 'Over there.' Blanc didn't understand where and looked around him.

'Over there,' Barnes whispered again.

Now Blanc could see what he meant. Huddled up, one arm contorted under him was Ames. Blanc let Barnes's head fall back on the coat.

He stood over Ames in horror. The eyes were wide open as if they'd rolled to the top of his head and stayed there bewildered. His hair was full of matted blood, beneath it his face seemed to have been rubbed in a green slime.

'We can still beat him ...' Barnes was saying deliriously.

'Who do you mean?' Blanc asked.

Barnes groaned.

'Who?' Blanc said again.

Barnes found enough strength to sneer. 'McCall.'

Blanc could hardly bear any more, the sight of Ames was more than he could stand. He was nauseated and staggered back to Barnes.

He knelt down beside him.

He tried sympathy. 'You'll be O.K.' He glanced back at the shape of Ames and then at the debris in the place.

'I'll get you out of here.'

'No.' Barnes' anger was fading. His face glistened red. He had lost a great deal of blood. He was dying alone and he knew it. Pretence was useless. He had traded with both sides and lost everything. Yet he still seemed to be raging, confident that he was pulling down everything with him before he lost consciousness for the last time.

'We'll destroy him, we'll destroy him. Destroy.'

Blanc watched him. It had seemed such a gentle face. Now, without glasses and his eyes screwed up in agony, Barnes looked wild. Once or twice his body shook with pain, or it could have been anger. There was nothing left to say. Barnes's muscles bunched up in his face and as if dictating a telegram he murmured without prompting,

'McCall shot him in the head point blank. He tried to hump Ames across to that ...'

He stopped.

'To what?' Blanc said.

'To that. Over there, next to Ames. It's a disused hatchway to the sewers. The water below. He gave up. Ames was too heavy.'

That explained the smell. McCall had tried to dump Ames in the sewers beneath.

'Who did *you* in?'

'Bloody hell, who do you think?'

'McCall?'

Barnes nodded.

Blanc leaned over him and put his arm under his neck once more. He looked towards the door and imagined that the whole basement area would be full of the putrid smell.

Barnes's forehead was running with sweat as well as blood. The mixture collected in drops and ran into Barnes's eyes. It was easier for him to keep them shut. He had lost the strength to shake the blood and sweat out.

Blanc stood up. He wondered if all corpses began to look alike. He stumbled over the mess on the floor and replaced the manhole cover. Far down below the water rushed on.

After he finally managed to drop the cover in place he went over to Barnes.

His face had relaxed, perhaps there was a trace of a smile on the mouth, but it might have been the inclination of his head.

It was all over.

For the second time in his life Blanc had seen someone die. Before it had been different—a young leering KGB official who deserved it. Barnes looked almost innocent as though he had lost ten years of his life.

It never occurred to Blanc as he looked down at the corpse that death was the most perfect disguise for a double agent. It provided a security that could never be broken.

Perhaps it was shock (he was never quite sure) but almost without realising it tears ran down his face. He stood there amongst the waste and the streaks of slime from the manhole and wept. The tears were salt and clean.

He had grown used to the stench of the sewers.

14

The new officers of the sub-section were careerists whose salaries went into insurance policies and mortgages; they read the *Financial Times* and the *Economist* because most of them had already invested a few hundred pounds in equities.

Security had become a fashionable subject for conversation; the cruelty and materialism reflected in one sort of fiction; the loneliness, dejection, the dust of another kind. The facts? 'Well, the facts,' Smith would say, assuming an air of professional pride, 'the facts are that we're technologists on very limited expenses; the game has changed, no romanticism now—it always leads to destruction.' It had become cosy because the older men had been recalled. It was somehow better for everyone that they should be pensioned off; no desk jobs, no roles (as they were called) on interview boards. So they had brought in the young men: from the universities with degrees in Languages or in Economics, some with a specialised knowledge of English Literature, who always wrote the best reports. It was less dramatic. Until a defection. That was when they got scared; as they did when the news of a double agent spread round in whispers, over drinks, in the corridors or in the lavatories. Then they all got scared.

Defections usually preceded other disappearances, ground agents would meet with familiar kinds of accidents.

What had never happened before was that someone at administrative level, highly respected even if not much liked, had shot somebody from the other side. Even Blanc had noticed that McCall had changed since the farmhouse. He had become sharper, more brittle. In most men this might have escaped notice. But in McCall, who was so relaxed, so self assured, so sure of himself and others around him, it was completely unexpected.

Marcia had telephoned Smith at his home when Blanc didn't return to his room after half an hour. And Smith had got out of bed and driven straight to the club with his hair unbrushed. The sub-section had let him use a car for the week so that, ostensibly, he could investigate immigration procedures at London Airport.

He found Blanc in his room.

'You'd better ring McCall,' he said nervously.

'No good from here,' Blanc said. 'The porter's a nosey bastard.'

So they went down to a callbox opposite the main bar. The porter woke up and realised something was going on and stood nonchalantly in the hall with mock efficiency all over him but just out of earshot of Smith's conversation.

He spoke to the sub-section. McCall wasn't there.

There was no reply from his hotel. The night porter must have left the switchboard. Smith dialled the sub-section a second time. But the girl at the other end wasn't co-operating.

'No one called McCall here, sir. This is the Overseas Board,' she whined.

'Put me through to the Duty Officer.' He had better luck with him. McCall *had* been there. But several hours ago. Apparently someone called Barnes had telephoned him to say that Donnelly had left London Airport alone on a flight to Montreal. McCall had been furious and had said that he was going out to check on Ames, Waterman and Barnes. Yes. He'd drawn a gun on signature. Yes. It was highly unusual. Yes. The Duty Officer had told him he couldn't have a gun on only two signatures. No. He hadn't rung in.

Smith swore at him and together with Blanc he went upstairs.

Smith told Marcia to stay where she was as he pulled on his coat and Blanc did likewise.

Then they ran downstairs.

McCall must have gone to Kew to complete the checkup. On Waterman.

They drove due south over Westminster Bridge. Its lights were shrouded in fog and they couldn't see the river.

Smith turned right towards a silent and sleeping Battersea. Normally he would not have driven so fast, he wouldn't have dared to in an official car. He held the steering wheel tightly as if he believed he could force the tyres to grip harder on the hard ridges of frozen slush.

In Putney he braked too late at some traffic lights and cursed as the car skidded into the middle of the crossing. But there was no one else on the road and he accelerated violently so that the car swung out sideways at the back. Somehow it straightened out.

'We should make Waterman's place in about thirty minutes,' he said between his teeth, 'if it doesn't get any thicker.' Nearer Richmond the fog closed right in on them and they could see it caught and swirling in the headlights.

Smith had pet theories about routes out of London. It was better in bad weather to go westwards on the other side of the river. The fog was easier there. But for once his theory had let him down.

Smith's uneasiness ran deeper than the mere safety of his car: why should McCall have taken the initiative on his own to kill Ames and Barnes. If there *was* a reason, why had he kept it to himself?

It was highly irregular.

Blanc had his own opinion. McCall would have realised that it was a matter of timing. No arrests could be made until there was conclusive evidence of a conspiracy, until Donnelly and the others had begun to close in on their unknown victims.

It would be then that McCall would strike. Very fast — because the four men would be operating on the pickpocket theory. (One man engaged the victim in conversation and innocent banter whilst another dipped his hand in the bag, removed the purse or wallet, passed it in a split second to a third man who did the same to a fourth. The cover was a market and if a detective *was* watching he'd have to keep his eyes on all four men at once. Impossible.) Thus Margot was out of it. Donnelly was the first decoy and had already left the country. Ames, now dead, would have taken the weapons because there hadn't been any in the basement. And Waterman would be waiting in the Keeper's Lodge in the Royal Botanical Gardens at Kew all ready to go with the arms; a shot in a crowd, a body pushed under a tube train. He would leave for Montreal too. Quietly. So why had McCall shot Ames and Barnes so soon? If he didn't get to Waterman it would have been all for nothing. So why had Richard McCall panicked?

Blanc told Smith his reasoning. Smith believed it. It was perfectly true that McCall had been very distraught for some time. In a man like McCall it was very noticeable simply because it was so unusual.

'He called in all the vetting files on you before he told you Barnes was the double agent. He insisted that he see you alone with Barnes. He was going to confront him with the beating up.'

'The meeting just petered out though,' Blanc said. 'McCall didn't even give me any proper instructions. Apart from anything else he forgot to tell me the basement was an armoury.'

The car was skidding on the ice.

'Keep going, and don't change gear,' Blanc said sharply. He rubbed the inside of the windscreen with his cuff.

Beyond Richmond the fog began to lift. They followed the road along the high boundary wall of Kew Gardens for nearly a mile, and Smith turned off the main road and drove down the side of Kew Green towards the river.

There were no lights on in the houses.

They looked out over the green and its snow was untouched and luminous. It made the houses look as though they belonged to a deserted child's nursery.

The fog had cleared without their noticing it.

Thick and tangled snow-covered ivy spread over the walls of Ferry Lane like a protective wire mesh.

There was an alley at the side of the house with two old bicycles propped against each other at the end of it. Beyond that and almost hidden was the door to Waterman's house.

Smith and Blanc breathed out into the freezing cold. They had been so intent on finding the door that once they found it they weren't sure whether to press the bell or just break in. They had both expected to see lights on, to see some sign that McCall was in there with Waterman.

A jet roared overhead, the noise shivered above the clouds and lifting fog. Then as if harnessing its power for a final burst, the jet roared again and began to fade as it lowered itself towards the airport.

'Get up on the lean-to,' Smith said. 'See if there's a ground-floor window you can get in through.'

Blanc walked with deliberate calmness to the end of the alley and swung himself up onto a corrugated iron roof a few feet off the ground. The cold numbed his hands.

'What can you see?' Smith said, looking up.

'Looks as though the windows are shuttered. Most of them at any rate. There's a small one I could see something through.'

'Go on. Fast. I'll wait here.'

Blanc let himself drop into the garden, his shoes sinking into the frozen snow. If McCall was there perhaps he was waiting for them. He would have guessed that they would follow him. Blanc thought it odd that his present fear originated in uncertainty : the house might reveal more about McCall, that he had turned tail. On the other hand it might be that McCall was cornered.

He made no attempt to approach the house like a petty thief. He walked quickly, too quickly, along the side of a snow-covered rose bed. The bushes had been pruned harshly and looked like unnatural stumps, black and rather vicious. His footsteps seemed muted underneath him in the silence, as though the snow had smothered the sounds of night, having already killed off nature in the trimmed and tended flowerbeds. He almost expected to hear the noise.

He stopped.

'Smith?' He's followed me over the wall, he thought. He's seen someone in the house.

Smith was silent.

'Smith, are you there?' He waited and heard something scurry in the rhododendrons. He listened and heard the scurry again, then it stopped. Nothing. If Smith was moving around he should keep quiet about it.

He walked on, more slowly this time.

Another jet, higher than the last, seemed suspended above by its blast, wavering and jumping a little. He looked up. The clouds were lifting. The windows were shuttered inside, below them was a gap and the folds of heavy lined curtains drawn inside the room. He pressed his face against the cold glass, his breath leaving expanding circles of moisture which began to drip at the edges. It was pointless. He could see nothing except the shutters. Impatient, he ran across the snow to the far side of the house that faced the garden; again he peered inside, rubbing away the traces of his breath. This was the kitchen, and with the colourless light from the snow he could see the kitchen furniture in the gloom. A broad wooden table with crockery on it, a coffee pot with an electric wire dangling over the table's edge, boxes of cereal and ready-cut bread in an opened packet.

He looked up to the window above; the house was in darkness. Peering out across the garden he noticed a black mound in the snow, something dropped in a hurry.

He walked across the lawn, where the snow was loose and without a crust. It puffed up around his feet as he walked and he left long footprints behind him. A pigeon, dead and stiff, was pointing its rootlike legs up into the air as if in pleading to be taken into the warmth, a plea for one last chance. No one had seen it and now it was part of the rigid white and black garden.

Smith was standing underneath the wall.

'Nothing. No one there,' Blanc said. 'Someone had breakfast in the kitchen. Could have been today or yesterday, can't tell. Rest of the place is shuttered, curtains drawn.'

'What about upstairs?'

'No lights. Nothing. Waterman'll be in bed anyway.'

'I doubt it. Not after tonight. Not after Ames. Certainly not if McCall's in there too.'

Smith had done up all the buttons of his jacket, looking like a schoolboy.

'We'd better go in.'

Blanc was still on the wall above the lean-to. 'We can break the glass. Give me a hand.' He pulled Smith up onto the wall and they dropped down into the snow, banging into each other.

They walked together past the larger windows and towards the smaller one beyond.

Then Smith reached for Blanc's coat.

A door slammed.

It came from somewhere out of sight in front of them at the side of the house, and then footsteps, regular and firm, came towards them.

There was only one man.

A figure in a long greatcoat, keys jingling in his pockets. 'Stay where you are,' he said.

Blanc and Smith said nothing.

'What do you want?'

'We're looking for Mr Dennis Waterman.' Smith said softly.

'Are you friends of his?' It seemed irrelevant, and Blanc, eager to answer, to say something, replied, 'Yes, old friends.'

'We'll see,' the man said, 'Just come with me.'

They followed him round the side of the house and through the back door of a small cottage adjoining the larger house.

They stood in the hallway. The man was smoothfaced and younger than he had seemed outside.

'I'm the duty keeper,' he said, pushing his hands into the pockets of his coat. 'If you want to see Mr Waterman you ask me.'

'We do,' Smith said.

'You can wait till morning.'

'Let's say we make a compromise. You tell us if Mr Waterman's in the house, if there's anyone with him.'

'There isn't.'

'You mean no one at all?'

'No one at all. Mr Waterman left this morning.'

'Where?'

'Why do you want to know?'

'All right,' Smith said with resignation. He brought out a transparent plastic envelope from his inside pocket. 'Now, you answer my questions, please. Quickly.'

The man was impressed by the card, to him it seemed that officialdom with cards countersigned twice and with a photograph on them, represented an authority superior to his long blue coat, pale blue shirt and greasy black tie with its small sharp knot.

'Would you like some tea?'

'All right.' Smith knew he had succeeded. 'Thanks.'

They sat on high uncomfortable chairs in the front room. The man took off his coat and underneath it was a tunic of the same dark blue which he hadn't bothered to do up. Blanc let Smith ask the questions.

'Mr Waterman's gone. He left this morning. Hounslow Taxis took him to the airport. He's gone to Montreal.'

'How long for?'

'I don't know.'

'Didn't he tell you?'

'There's no reason why he should. I'm just a keeper.'

'Weren't you asleep then, if you were off duty?'

'He left just after I came off, at eight. I saw him go.'

'What did he say?'

'Nothing. He didn't notice me.'

'Isn't there someone he'd tell if he was leaving?'

'His office, perhaps. But he's a law to himself, Mr Waterman. He never says much. Never has. Not since I've been here and it's ten years, no eleven years now.'

'Why do you think he's gone to Montreal?'

'Why should I know? I'm just a keeper. I only ever passed the time of day with him recently.' Smith walked across the front room to the window and parted the curtains. The man was still talking. 'He used to have a real interest in the staff did Mr Waterman and I was something special. It sounds ...' he broke off.

Smith watched the condensation running down onto the window ledge. 'Odd,' said Smith, finishing the sentence.

'Well, I've lived here next to Mr Waterman all this time ...' the man lingered reluctantly, sensing that a chapter had been closed and that he hadn't been told. He was staring at the carpet. There was no reason why Waterman should have told him he was leaving. Had they met casually between their houses he might have told him just to pass over the inconvenience of the encounter and the need to make some conversation. The shared confidences which Waterman imparted at such times gave the man a sense of importance, the feeling that he was involved in Waterman's working routine; and however superficial they might have been, they gave him a degree of self-respect which he valued.

'He'll be back,' the man said.

He reached into his pocket for a tin, folding some tobacco into a small metal and rubber contraption for rolling cigarettes. 'He'll be back; they're redoing the tropical plant houses—the ventilation and suchlike. They have to have Mr Waterman there. Then there's the people coming to see him, they come from all over.'

It seemed to Smith that the man's need to reassure himself of Waterman's return implied doubt about it. His own presence, along with Blanc's, the official identity card, the visit in the middle of the night; all of this made him doubtful. And when his self-made cigarette was ready he looked up.

'Why do you want to see him, anyway?'

'Just a routine check.'

'The police?'

'Sort of, with an offer of assistance.'

'I'd like to help you, but there's nothing I can do for you.'

'There's nothing you *can* do, or you *want* to do?'

'There's nothing I can do.'

'What about the house? We could have a quick look inside.'

'You'll have to have his permission.'

'Whose?'

'Mr Waterman's.'

'Perhaps we could leave a message for him inside.'

The man persisted. 'You can leave it with me.'

'We'll send it then,' offered Smith.

'I'd like to let you into the house.' He was trying to soften his authority without losing it. 'But I can't.'

'I understand,' Smith said. 'There's nothing you want to tell us? About Mr Waterman?'

'No.' The man was trying to please them, and had second thoughts.

'There might be something you'd notice and I wouldn't.'

140

'Maybe,' Smith said, 'but you're used to what goes on here. You're the one who'd notice.'

'There's nothing.'

'Well at least Mr Waterman will be pleased there's nothing.' Smith regretted the patronising tone of his remark. They stood up, the man pulling on his greatcoat and shrugging his shoulders to make it fit more comfortably. He turned up his collar against his neck, making his hair stick out at the back. 'I'll show you the way out. I'll have to take you to the main gate. You can't leave the way you came in, and you can't go through the house. I've no keys.'

'You mean to say you've no keys for Mr Waterman's place?'

'None that can let you out through the house.'

The sky had cleared and opened up above them. The three of them walked together through the gardens. In the blue light the plants and trees looked dead or dying, as if they were fighting for survival in the cold, the sap freezing from the roots upwards.

Once or twice Blanc touched a finger to his cheek and could hardly feel it. They walked quickly, slipping now and again on the frozen path. They took a short cut across a wide lawn, leaving footsteps elongated in the snow.

They didn't look up.

If they had they would have seen Sirius teasing and twinkling above them and changing its colour from red to emerald, a part of the winter sky that went unnoticed. The man in his greatcoat would not see the stars through his glasses, he looked short-sighted. Blanc thought he looked like a portrait he had once seen of Gerard Manley Hopkins who couldn't see the stars either :

> Sky peak'd with tiny flames.
> Stars like tiny-spoked wheels of fire.

But none of them looked up.

Almost as an afterthought; like a midge rising when the wind goes down, part of the unpleasantness of summer which is somehow forgotten in the cold, the man called to them through the gate as he locked it after them:

'Someone called to see Mr Waterman earlier, this evening. A man alone. He rang the bell, walked round the outside of the house much like yourselves, then he left before I could speak to him. I shouted after him, he didn't stop.'

Smith turned, 'When was that?'

'I don't remember.'

'Try, man. *Try to remember.*'

'An hour or so before you came.'

Smith looked at Blanc. 'Did you notice anyone else's footprints outside the house?'

'No, they would have been covered up by the last fall of snow before we got there.'

Smith looked at the man again. 'Do you remember if it snowed between the other person's visit and ours?'

'It might have done. I think it did.'

'Thanks,' Smith called. He turned to Blanc, 'It *must* have been McCall.'

Inside the gardens the man made his way slowly back retracing the footprints. He tried to pick out his own by the print of the heavy rubber soles on his boots. The giant glass Palm House flickered in the dark. He could hear birds inside it twittering, trapped in the artificial heat and disturbed by the strangeness of the damp. The seasons were stopped in the hothouse, the water dripped down off the plants, the pipes hot and rusting like a vast and unhygienic incubator. The sky had opened up, the stars shining and naked. In summer it would have been dawn, the time of the birds, a kind of playtime beloved of children's dreams; the flowers tight and ready for the sun. Like all park attendants the man's mind was used to wandering and had relinquished the present for nostalgia. He did what he was told and only lived dangerously in his dreams. No one could tell him what to dream. He had already forgotten Waterman and the visitors.

15

Smith drove back to London recklessly. He was pale and angry. He told Blanc that something had gone wrong and he wasn't sure what; it was all very unsatisfactory. For the first time he confided in Blanc. What had begun as a well researched, methodical investigation of four men had now gone off the rails. Donnelly had left the country and had been followed by Waterman, at least if the keeper could be believed.

There was no reason to doubt his story.

The plan to break Donnelly's cell, his tight and well disguised operation, had been overtaken. Two of the quarries were dead. Margot murdered and no one knew who had done it. Ames shot, along with Barnes, by McCall. This was the bad feature. There would be a great deal of answering to be done. The only thought which gave him some pleasure, and it was a guilty pleasure, was that at least it had been McCall, his superior officer, who had bungled and not himself.

Neither of them had slept. Blanc's head slumped forwards onto his chest, once or twice he sat up with a start. It should have been so easy. Respectable backgrounds, a great deal known already. Quiet, orderly arrests by the Special Branch when the time came. A trial in camera. Punitive sentences. Blanc paid off, the files closed. Instead there was a mess.

'I'm not waiting till morning,' Smith said, 'I'm going to phone McCall, we should have rung him before.'

'That's the point,' Blanc said, 'you don't know where he is.'

'No. The sub-section will though.'

He pulled the car into the kerb in the Cromwell Road and went into a call box. Blanc watched him feed a sixpence into the box, and then lean on a pile of directories and cross

143

his legs. The box began to steam up and he saw Smith shift his stance from one side to the other.

Smith, a permanent member of the sub-section, did have a telephone number for McCall. It was a hotel off Oxford Street. There was no need to call the department at all. He cursed himself for not having got through to McCall earlier; on the other hand it was agreed that he shouldn't be telephoned at his hotel and anyway he hadn't been there. He had some difficulty in getting the night porter to answer and was about to give up when he answered.

'Room 360 please.'

'Is that the police?' a voice asked.

Smith hesitated, 'Yes,' he lied. '360 please.'

'Put you through.'

Another voice came on the line.

'Yes.'

'Who's that?'

'Bell. Special Branch.'

'Ah Mr Bell. Could I speak to Mr Richard McCall please?'

'Who's speaking?'

'Francis Smith. I'm a colleague of Mr McCall's.' Smith gripped the receiver tightly and peered out through the misted glass of the call box.

'I'm very sorry to have to tell you that Mr McCall's dead.'

Smith was silent and breathed out, stooping as his lungs emptied.

'Dead?'

'I'm afraid so.'

'When did he die?'

'About two hours ago. He was shot.'

'Can you tell me anything more?'

'There's not much more to say, sir, is there? If you're a colleague of his maybe you could come over here.'

'All right. In about twenty minutes.'

Blanc woke the next morning with a sense of failure and confusion. Marcia didn't come. Like everyone else she would know what to do in an emergency.

McCall was dead. His work, like Blanc's, was unfinished. No one could really say why. McCall had dealt in secrets and his collection had died with him. He had made a gruesome sight in the hotel room, it would be a night the hotel staff would long remember; in a determined way they would make sure that everyone remembered. In the hotel at least the history of McCall began with his death. Terrible descriptions of his head blown apart and deformed by a gun blast, the mouth open and torn as if gashed by some monstrous butcher's hook.

There was no family to identify the body. A senior officer would do that. With his bowler hat held across his chest in civilian dress salute, a tight sharp umbrella gripped firmly in the other hand at his side, he would say 'Yes'. And then turning brusquely on his heel he would disappear somewhere in London. His name would be a linear scrawl at the bottom of a *Special Branch Form of Identification.*

Death administers a peculiar chemistry over reputation, like the memory of uncomfortable holidays recalled with photographs; the blue skies, encounters, roadside halts. The rest of it, the arguments, irritability, petty observations— they are all forgotten. So too with McCall.

Blanc pitied his gamesmanship. He saw the dangers of the will to overcome 'because it's there' and the futility which escaped precise definition. It was romantic and dangerous.

Now there would be the knock on his door. Busek.

Blanc lay in bed feeling sticky and unwashed.

He shut his eyes and pulled up the sheets.

Then inevitably the knock. Someone was calling his name from the corridor.

'All right,' Blanc said wearily. 'Hold on.'

It sounded like the porter.

'There's someone to see you. In the front hall. A Mr Murdoch.'

'Who?'

'Mr Murdoch.'

Blanc recognised the beret.

Murdoch was holding it in both hands in a parody of ecclesiastical gesture. He looked different from the man who had directed him in the wind to Jean Mungo. He was pale and shabby.

Blanc was unshaven. They both seemed out of place, and the Royal Services Club felt terribly stale.

Murdoch held out his hand.

'I expect you're surprised to see me.'

'Yes,' said Blanc.

'Well. Perhaps we could find somewhere to talk alone.'

'Here?'

'I thought we could find a Lyons. A café or something.'

'Will they be open yet?'

'Oh I expect so.' Murdoch indicated the door. 'Up in Piccadilly, there must be somewhere.'

The porter glanced up at them as they left.

'It's very sad.'

'Yes,' Blanc said. 'You knew him really rather well.'

'Professionally, through the parish.'

'Ah.'

They didn't find a Lyons, and instead they made their way together to Jermyn Street and found a Trattoria. It couldn't have been more than half past eight and the street was empty. So too was the Trattoria, which had only just opened. There were rich coloured cakes in the windows on glass trays. And inside a coffee machine let out a hiss of steam.

They sat alone in the corner.

Murdoch sipped loudly at his coffee and ordered a large piece of wet looking chocolate cake.

He wiped his hands on a napkin and reached into his coat pocket. He brought out a neck chain and played with it in his hands.

'So what is it you want?' Blanc asked.

'This is yours.' He handed Blanc the neck chain. Attached to the smooth and fine gold links was a St Christopher medallion. 'Richard asked me to give you this if anything happened to him....'

Murdoch brushed the napkin across his face, dabbing at the corners of his mouth where chocolate had collected. 'He gave it me some weeks ago. There were no relations. Some cousins I think somewhere. But they didn't mean anything to him.'

'Why should he give this to me?'

146

'I think in a way he had you on his mind.'

'I didn't think he was religious.'

'It wasn't so much that he was religious. I mean, he wasn't interested in the Church. More just in God ... Anyhow he had a conscience.' Murdoch paused. 'And ... I'm not sure how to put it. Let's say it got the better of him. It defeated him. It ultimately defeated him.'

'What is it you're trying to tell me?'

'Precisely that.'

'That McCall's conscience defeated him? It's absurd.'

'No. Not really.'

'Even so, I'm not sure what all this has got to do with me. I mean McCall only died last night. He was murdered in an hotel room in Oxford Street.'

'Do you think so?'

'Yes. I suppose you know who did it?'

'I'm not a detective.'

'Neither am I. But you've come all the way from Swindon to give me this medallion. And you were the person who told McCall that I'd gone off with Jean Mungo. You were fairly directly involved in that.'

Murdoch let Blanc go on, watching him working himself up.

'And you know what happened to her ... strangled, beaten up, terrified by thugs. She died alone in a warehouse—a disused government railway warehouse. It stinks. It's as bad as Russia. Worse. And you a priest, a Church man—muddled up in this. I suppose you'll get a medal.'

Murdoch sat back as far as he could on the small wall bench.

He stretched out his hands, palms down. Then he rearranged the cup and saucer in front of him.

'I'm not here because anyone told me to be. I don't have to answer to officialdom.'

'Well then. Why are you here?'

Murdoch was pressing his fingers on the crumbs. He looked out into the street. Then he said, 'I've more to tell you. You'll do well to learn some patience.'

He waved at the man behind the coffee machine.

'Two more please. And another piece of cake.'

Blanc was becoming impatient at Murdoch's incredible coolness.

'Come on then,' Blanc said sharply.

Murdoch shrugged.

'I believe I know what you're thinking. It's only natural, I suppose. Let me start at the beginning. Richard told me to if anything happened.'

'All right,' said Blanc.

'The farmhouse outside Swindon was used three times during the last few years by the Foreign Office. They bought a twenty-year lease with a clause in it which allowed them to ask, rather insist, that the tenants leave directly they were asked to. The first time it happened the tenants came to me to protest. I took up their cause. That was how I came into contact with Richard. After that we got to know each other quite well. Whenever he came into Swindon to collect his official papers from the station he'd call in on me. We talked about politics and about the countryside and the dog. He was very fond of the dog. Whenever he left the farmhouse to come to London he left it with me. It's at home now. The spaniel. You remember it?'

'Yes. I remember it.'

'Well. Whenever he came to see me he talked about these things, never about his work. I understood. I realised he couldn't say much about it. Then suddenly all that changed. He opened up. He wanted to talk. I'm not sure exactly why. Never will be. It may have been a delayed reaction to his wife's death, a sudden need to unburden himself. He used to go to Bicester to visit the grave. They buried her near her birthplace. We had long discussions about the after-life. It's usual for widowers to want to talk about it. Invariably they come to believe in it that way. He wanted to. Badly. Even if for the wrong reasons. But he never quite could. And he became distraught about it. As if he'd been cheated of something which others obtained quite easily. First of all he thought he'd been robbed of something. Then he came to think he had a shortcoming. An inadequacy. That's what he called it. I did what I could. And our conversations seemed to help him.'

Blanc was by now infuriated.

'What *has* this got to do with me? It's a breach of confidence.'

'No. It's not a breach of confidence.'

'Well what the hell is it? Look you're wasting my time. And your own.'

'Look,' Murdoch said firmly. 'He wanted me to tell you.'

'Don't be ridiculous. You could tell his office.'

'No I could not.'

'Why not?'

'I'll come to it. Last year two spies were released from Parkhurst. McCall was sent to question them before they left the country. He spent a week down there. It's a kind of convention that spies aren't released unless they make the bargain good with information. It's not just a question of releasing someone held by the other side.'

'How do you know that?'

'Never mind.'

'McCall told you?'

'As a matter of fact yes, he did. And I didn't stop him. I've heard worse things. It seemed to help him. During the interrogations at Parkhurst, it emerged indirectly, that the new post-Philby organisation of the Security Services was proving effective. Information was, so to speak, being kept intact. But there was a new danger: of assassinations. Do you know about it?'

'You mean assassination scares?'

'No. Assassinations proper. There were plans in existence for several. The spies were offered their release if they would reveal details. It was as simple as that. And, as it emerged, as foolish.'

'Why?'

'I'll come to that. They mentioned four men, all of whom were already under suspicion of one sort or another. The Security Services had been on to them for some months. Maybe years. But no one knew *who* the assassination targets were. Then Embassy Officials intervened and automatically the spies shut up like clams. So an investigation into the four men was begun. And, as you know well enough, you were recruited as the person to plant the devices. There was an internal departmental dispute about this. But McCall gained the advantage. Then the visa question came up. McCall fixed it. Remember?'

'Of course.'

'McCall and Smith stepped in. You were ideal material. But in Swindon, something went wrong. First of all Jean Mungo ...'

'She was murdered.'

'I know. By McCall. He'd done that sort of thing before. But he was past it. Killing in cold blood eventually takes its toll on the killer. And that it was a young girl, a very young girl, began to destroy McCall. He was already cracking up, and he felt he had to make amends. He couldn't see her parents. So he asked me at least to tell you his real attitude. You called him a bastard and it sunk in.'

'It makes no difference.'

'Be that as it may. Then there was the problem of Barnes.'

'He was murdered too.'

'I know. He was shot by McCall because he was sure Barnes was the double agent. In the sub-section they diverted attention or rather suspicion onto you. Simply to let Barnes think no one suspected *him*. But McCall panicked. And he shot him in the act. And Ames got it too.'

'But he was never even tried.'

'I know.'

'But why, why shoot him?'

'Time was one factor. It was running out. Anyhow the subversion ran deep. The four men, excluding Barnes, were professional men. Operating together they could piece together information. Technological, political and so on. It was easy for them.'

'All right. McCall obviously told you a great deal. But where does it get us. Look, time's short....' Blanc's patience was being strained. They'd been there over half an hour. He must see Smith.

'Just let me finish. No one actually believed the stories of the spies, that they were part of the assassination syndicate. Only McCall. He believed it. Then things went wrong for both sides. First Jean Mungo on the one hand, then Margot on the other. It all began to play on McCall's mind. He was tortured by it. Didn't you see?'

150

'Not that I can remember,' Blanc hedged.

'McCall was reprimanded for the Mungo killing. Then he realised something else. He should never have been sent to interrogate the spies. They were being sent home. As hardened professionals they would remember who he was. That was what was foolish. His cover was blown. McCall saw the mistake, but it was too late. He was losing control of himself. Then Donnelly left the country; they couldn't stop him. McCall found Ames and Barnes in the weapon store. But the weapons had gone. McCall knew that he was beaten, that the others knew Margot had called their cards and so they passed the weapons on. Not just one assassination was planned but several. McCall then went to find Waterman. But when he got to Kew, Waterman had gone. So he returned to his hotel.'

'How do you know all this? McCall can't have told you that he had returned to his hotel room.'

'Because,' he said, 'human vanity is curious. Particularly when the person concerned is desperate. When he's beaten.'

'What are you trying to tell me then?'

'Richard telephoned me last night when he returned to his hotel. He told me everything I've told you. He told me that you were at the club; that he'd tried to telephone you there but you were out. When he finished speaking with me I too tried to telephone you. But you still hadn't got back. Richard had asked me to thank you.'

'He *knew* that they'd get him?'

'In a way.'

'So they did murder him.'

'No. Not so.'

'Well, who did?'

'He knew that they'd get him. In a way. He shot himself.'

Once more Murdoch dabbed his fingers on the crumbs. One by one he was transferring them from the plastic table to the plate in front of him.

'I suppose your sub-section knows about their plans?' he said.

'Yes. They know quite a bit.'

'Who the targets are?'

'I don't think so.'

'Or who they've handed the weapons to?'

'I'm not sure.'

'But *surely* you know.'

'It's not the kind of thing they tell me.'

'Are you *sure*?'

Blanc wondered why Murdoch would want to know.

'Are you quite sure?' Murdoch asked again.

'Yes.'

Murdoch's face seemed to pale. He scratched the table.

No one else had come in. The place was empty. Even the man behind the counter had gone.

'Finally, Blanc,' Murdoch said nervously, 'there's the question of Busek. The KGB. Richard asked me to help you. I'll contact you at the club. Have you sorted it out?'

'Not really.'

'What will you do now?' Murdoch asked him.

'Go back to where I was before. Avoid Busek. And continue my research. It's behindhand. But if my work for McCall is finished ...'

Blanc didn't complete the sentence. He just said, 'I suppose both sides lost.'

'I'll be in touch. Soon,' said Murdoch. 'There are other things to talk over.'

They walked to the door. The morning was overcast. As Murdoch stepped onto the pavement the plate glass door swung shut abruptly between them.

Blanc felt someone pull him violently backwards.

'Get down.'

Blanc went to his knees instinctively.

'On your face. On your bloody face!'

Blanc threw himself forwards and was pulled the rest of the way down.

'Stay where you are!' The shouts must have come from behind him but there were others coming from the other side of the street.

Shouts were compressed into a shriek and crashing, splintering glass. The noise was deafening. From left to right, diagonally, a stream of bullets smashed into the window and across the door thrown open by the impact.

Cakes toppled off trays as they collapsed. Crockery slewed

off a table under the window.

The display lights flashed puffing out blue smoke.

Blanc had kept his eyes on Murdoch. 'You can't do it to him,' Blanc was yelling. 'No more, stop it.' But Murdoch was forced back by a great pressure into the doorway. His head shook with several spasms from side to side and then bent backwards.

He didn't scream. He just sagged a little and toppled forwards into the street.

Two men ran forward from a car parked opposite. People were coming out of the shops to look. Just a few of them, open mouthed and rigid.

Murdoch's body was dragged across the road trailing blood, to an official black saloon with a radio aerial. It drove off, a rear door still open, towards St James's. The door was closed.

Blanc was on his feet. It had taken two minutes. No longer than two minutes.

It was Francis Smith who had pulled him to the floor of the café and who led him shaking and beaten to the office building in Victoria—the offices of the sub-section.

* * *

A desperate and almost brilliant attempt to deceive was how Francis Smith summed up Waterman's impersonation of Murdoch.

'It was a gamble and it worked. Up to a point. You *had* seen Murdoch once, but very briefly. So briefly that you would have only remembered the beret. Presumably you did?'

'Yes, although Murdoch's manner was more relaxed.'

'Waterman couldn't leave until he had found out precisely how much we knew. If, for example, we had discovered where the contents of the makeshift arms store had been taken.'

Smith walked across the office to a map on the wall. 'And we still don't know. All we've managed to do is smash Donnelly's cell. And we've lost one of our best men in the process.'

Blanc had spent the remainder of the morning telling and retelling the account of his meeting with Waterman.

His suspicions had never been aroused. He had been completely duped.

A secretary had been present to record every word of Blanc's account.

Smith explained that the medallion was not of course McCall's. Nor had he ever possessed one. It was quite true that he had murdered Jean Mungo. Donnelly's people had wired Murdoch's telephone. So everything McCall told his confessor just before he took his life was known to them. In such confessions the past is gone over in terrible detail, every shade of guilt is examined. McCall had delved deep into the past for Murdoch. And for Donnelly too.

The episode in Parkhurst was also true. And Barnes was a double agent, an ineffective one who was tolerated in order that the sub-section could feed false information to Donnelly.

'But surely,' Blanc insisted, 'Waterman could never have hoped to get away with it.'

'But he *did*,' Smith said. 'You *were* taken in.'

'All right. But how did you know Waterman had come to the club to see me?'

'We immediately had everyone involved watched after Richard's death. It's an emergency precaution. On the other hand even the best individual agent makes his final mistake. Usually when he's desperate. That's how we finally found Philby out. George Blake was caught in the same way. An agent on his last legs must find out how much his opponents know about him. Waterman tried like the others I've just mentioned. We guessed he'd contact you because he couldn't approach me. Barnes is dead and Marcia was too junior.'

Smith stood against the map on the wall. He couldn't disguise his pleasure.

'Why for God's sake,' Blanc asked, 'did you have to kill him?'

'There was no alternative. Eventually he'd be just another exchange bargain. He knew too much. We *had* to do it.'

'But why like that?' Blanc asked with disgust.

'Why not?'

Blanc sighed.

Smith sat down again behind his desk.

'There's only Donnelly now. And the Canadian police are already onto him. We'll get him somehow.'

154

'You must be making a mistake in killing like that.'

'No,' Smith was philosophical. 'It's the penalty we've had to pay for reorganisation. The Embassies and Intelligence Services on all sides have always dreaded that their men would be killed by the other side. Once you start there is no end to it.'

'And that's the stage you've now reached?'

'Yes. Regrettably. The cover is gang warfare. Or the unexplained killing which is very sudden. It'll be covered up. Murder can be disguised. The more public it is the easier it is to hide because details get lost in public enquiries. The only other effective guise is to get the victim to kill himself. Now you've seen both methods in operation. And there may be other killings too. We'll see.'

'What about Murdoch?'

'He's in Swindon with the spaniel. We'll let him keep it.'

* * *

During the weeks that followed Blanc searched the Press for the other shootings.

Three stood out.

A report in a lunch-time edition of the *Evening Standard* described the killing of a French diplomat; a first-secretary who was shot leaving a new block of flats in Brixton. Gang warfare.

Two days later a Foreign Office Official was found dead in St John's Wood. Armed Robbery. His body had lain in his flat for three days before it was discovered.

A week after that an 'officer' of the West German Embassy was shot in Brighton. Suspected armed robbery. Then all the reports ended. Nothing else appeared.

Blanc received a letter at the Royal Services Club which told him to report to the Immigration and Nationality Department at the Home Office in High Holborn to discuss his visa.

But before that he and Marcia took a train to Woking for the funeral of Richard McCall.

They were glad to be going in the opposite direction to the rush hour crowds outside Waterloo.

'You know, Marcia,' Blanc said, 'it's just like Prague. If all these people weren't late and had forgotten what time of day it was they couldn't find out.'

'Unless they looked at their watches.'

'Yes, but the shop windows are brightly lit. It's dark and cold, and the decorations are still in the windows.'

'They'd tell. Like animals that hibernate. They wake up at the right time.'

There were about half a dozen people at the graveside. The others besides Blanc, Marcia and Smith looked like businessmen.

As the service ended Blanc walked to the cemetery alone.

The 'businessmen' gave Smith and Marcia a lift back to London.

Blanc would go on the train. He was in no hurry.

It wasn't until the man in a heavy grey overcoat introduced himself at the gates to the cemetery that Blanc knew who he was.

'Jaromir Busek,' he said quietly.

In the January morning his face like Blanc's was drawn.

Also by Reg Gadney

Somewhere in England

He knew what would happen if it caught fire. Because once nitrate film begins to deteriorate it is described by the experts as 'sticky'...at this point it becomes highly explosive... Academic David Peto's research involves viewing hour-after-hour of Nazi propaganda films in a private archive on the desolate Suffolk coast. If that wasn't harrowing enough, an explosion in the film store drops Peto into the middle of a conspiracy involving Middle Eastern intelligence agencies and the sinister ODESSA organisation. Could he have inadvertently identified a wanted Nazi war criminal on one of the films? A war criminal now living 'somewhere in England'? Peto becomes ensnared in a dangerous game of hide-and-seek across London which culminates in an audacious burglary of the Imperial War Museum.

First published in 1971 and described by the New Statesman as: *'Tense, razor-sharp and excellent value'*

ISBN 9781909619197

Lightning Source UK Ltd.
Milton Keynes UK
UKHW02f2304040618
323718UK00007B/524/P